SPIRITUAL TRANSFORMATION
KEY TO VICTORY

SPIRITUAL TRANSFORMATION
KEY TO VICTORY

LYNDA STURDEVANT

ReadersMagnet, LLC

Spiritual Transformation: Key to Victory
Copyright © 2019 by Lynda Sturdevant

Published in the United States of America
ISBN Paperback: 978-1-949981-71-1
ISBN eBook: 978-1-949981-72-8

All rights reserved. No part of this publication may be reproduced, stored in a retrieval system or transmitted in any way by any means, electronic, mechanical, photocopy, recording or otherwise without the prior permission of the author except as provided by USA copyright law.

The Holy Bible, Authorized King James Version, Copyright 1945 by E World Publishing Company.

The opinions expressed by the author are not necessarily those of ReadersMagnet, LLC.

ReadersMagnet, LLC
10620 Treena Street, Suite 230 | San Diego, California, 92131 USA
1.619. 354. 2643 | www.readersmagnet.com

Book design copyright © 2019 by ReadersMagnet, LLC. All rights reserved.
Cover design by Ericka Walker
Interior design by Shemaryl Evans

CONTENTS

Introduction: Called To The Harvest 7
Lesson 1: Regeneration 9
Lesson 2: Doctrine of Baptisms 24
Lesson 3: The Holy Spirit 45
Lesson 4: Reasonable Service 56
Lesson 5: Experiencing God 72
Lesson 6: Spiritual Exercise 82
Lesson 7: Holiness 113
Lesson 8: Motivation of love 119
Lesson 9: Humility in Action 131
Lesson 10: The Abundant Life 143
Lesson 11: Gift of Faith 155
Lesson 12: Gifts of God 166
Lesson 13: Called to the Battle 192
Lesson 14: The Armor of God 208
Lesson 15: The Watchman 219
Lesson 16: Our Glorification 226

Afterword 245

INTRODUCTION

Called To The Harvest

Luk 10:2 Therefore said he unto them, The harvest truly *is* great, but the labourers *are* few: pray ye therefore the Lord of the harvest, that he would send forth labourers into his harvest.

THE OBJECTIVE OF THESE COURSES IS TO PROVIDE the foundational tools that will root and ground the believer in his faith and equip him for his work in the Last Harvest. It is not meant to be an exhaustive, comprehensive study but discipleship in the basic tenets of the Christian faith. As laborers together with God we out of necessity must be a disciple for we receive all our provision from the kingdom of God by faith. We learn to know God and hear him when we read his written word. Although we are laborers in God's fields, we must never forget that we also are God's husbandry: his farm, his cultivation. We are being built together for a habitation of God through the Spirit. Under Christ watchful care and the teaching of his word by the Spirit of God, we grow from glory to glory; from strength to strength. Understanding the principles of (1Co 3:7-8) will keep us focused on our need for him in all that we undertake in his Name. Whether we plant the seed or whether we water we are one, and it is God who deserves all the glory for he only can give the increase to our labor.

> **1Co 3:7** So then neither is he that planteth any thing, neither he that watereth; but **God that giveth the increase.**
>
> **1Co 3:8** Now he that planteth and he that watereth are one: and every man shall receive his own reward according to his own labour.

Keeping these principles toward God and one another will help guard against foolish pride and temptation to exalt ourselves. Jesus Christ is the Cornerstone, the foundation of the Church whom the whole building is built upon and framed around, not us. We must be cautious of how we build upon his foundation. We shall receive rewards according to our labor and how we build upon the foundation of our faith. Let us pray that we are counted worthy of God's calling. We shall see his purpose accomplished in our lives by the mighty power of Christ Jesus.

LESSON 1

Regeneration

OBJECTIVE: Develop an understanding of the transformation process of spiritual regeneration.

REGENERATION & RENEWING

- generation—the propagation of living organisms, procreation.
- regeneration—spiritual rebirth.

> **Gen 1:27** So God created man in his *own* image, in the image of God created he him; male and female created he them.

> **Gen 1:28** And God blessed them, and God said unto them, **Be fruitful, and multiply, and replenish the earth, and subdue it: and have dominion** over the fish of the sea, and over the fowl of the air, and over every living thing that moveth upon the earth.

The Hebrew word rendered replenish in this KJV text is the old English word for fill. In our current culture, the word replenish has been changed to mean refill. Adam and Eve are the original inhabitants of the earth. God formed the first man Adam from the dust of the ground in his likeness and his image (Gen 2:7). Out of all God's creation, there was none found that was comparable to Adam for a mate. So, God put Adam to sleep, took a rib from his side, and formed a woman. The woman was created to be Adam's counterpart and helper (Gen 2:22).

God created them male and female and blessed them and gave them dominion and told them to **be fruitful and multiply and fill the earth**. He made them male and female to have an intimate relationship and to procreate, forming the family unit. God called them both by the name of Adam. After the fall, Adam called his wife Eve which means the mother of all living (Gen 3:20). All generations of humanity are the offspring of Adam and Eve inheriting their fallen nature.

> Rom 5:12   Wherefore, as **by one man sin entered into the world,** and death by sin; and so death passed upon all men, for that **all have sinned**:

When Adam sinned, it corrupted all generations that followed with a sin nature. God's son came from heaven to become flesh that he might destroy the works of the devil and transform the nature of man, reversing the effects of the fall of the first Adam. The first Adam was a living soul, the last Adam, a life-giving spirit.

- **FYI-TRANSFORMATION**-IN MOLECULAR BIOLOGY TRANSFORMATION IS THE GENETIC ALTERATION OF A CELL RESULTING FROM THE DIRECT UPTAKE AND **INCORPORATION OF EXOGENOUS (OUTSIDE) MATERIAL** FROM IT'S SURROUNDINGS THROUGH THE CELL MEMBRANE.

(Exogenous variable—an independent variable that affects the model without being affected by it)

(Wikipedia)

There were examples of molecular transformation when Jesus ministered. From his touch or spoken word virtue was transferred from Jesus into the person. Their biology was genetically altered; transformed because of the righteousness incorporated into their cells, yet Jesus was not affected by their words or touch. Some examples are: in the woman with the issue of blood (Mar 5:25-30); the leper (Mat 8:2-3); a gentile woman's daughter vexed with a devil (Mar 7:25-30). The Pharisees avoided touching people because they feared being defiled by them, but Jesus was not afraid of being contaminated. Although flesh, Jesus was the Holy One born of a virgin and over whom the effects of sin had no power.

This principle of transformation in the physical realm is a type of transformation in the spiritual realm. Man was dead in trespasses and sins and needed forgiveness, regeneration and renewal (Eph 2:1, Tit 3:5). All mankind and his offspring (seed) were corrupted because of the sin of Adam. If not for God's mercy there would be no hope. He sent mankind a savior, an outside variable that could affect man without man's sin affecting him: one who Satan had no place in. **Jesus conquered sin** by being obedient unto death, and **then he conquered death** and rose the third day. Death could not hold him without sin's grip (Php 2:8; Act 2:24).

Man's soul had to be atoned for with a perfect sacrifice before he could be regenerated (given new life). Once the atonement was made forgiveness is available for those who put their faith in Christ, and they are washed in the blood of his sacrifice and in the waters of his word by the Holy Spirit.

In essence, the life of the Son of God who came down from above to become flesh is the exogenous (outside) material incorporated into the spirit of those who believe; His blood cleansing and His Spirit reproducing His life within making a new creation.

- Principle: A seed brings forth after its own kind (Gen 1: 11-12, 20-21, 24-28).

There is a principle of the seed found in Genesis 1 which says that a seed brings forth after its kind. Faith began as an incorruptible seed; The Word of God which is Spirit and Life. The word like a seed becomes planted within our hearts, and we are born again by that word (1 Pet 1:23). We are saved by the washing of regeneration (spiritual rebirth) and the renewal power of the Holy Ghost (Tit 3:5). Christ gives his life to man, making him a new creation. We are baptized into Christ body and become flesh of his flesh and bone of his bone (Eph 5:30). It is by God's power alone that the new birth and oneness with Christ is possible.

> **Tit 3:5** Not by works of righteousness which we have done, but according to his mercy **he saved us, by the washing of regeneration**, and **renewing of the Holy Ghost**.

- regeneration—spiritual rebirth.
- renewing—renovation.

THE ATONEMENT

- atonement—exchange, restoration and reconciliation (Ro 5:8-11)

> **Lev 17:11** For the **life of the flesh** *is* **in the blood**: and I have given it to you upon the altar to make an atonement for your souls: for **it** *is* **the blood** *that* **maketh an atonement for the soul.**

- Principle: The life of the flesh is in the blood (Lev 17:11).

- Principle: Blood is given to make atonement for the soul (Lev 17:11).

JUSTIFIED BY HIS BLOOD

- justified—render just or innocent, free, righteous.

> **Isa 53:11** He shall see of the travail of his soul, *and* shall be satisfied: by his knowledge shall my righteous servant **justify many; for he shall bear their iniquities.**
>
> **Rom 5:9** Much more then, being now **justified by his blood**, we shall be saved from wrath through him.
>
> **Rom 5:10** For if, when we were enemies, we were reconciled to God by the death of his Son, much more, being reconciled, we shall be saved by his life.
>
> **Rom 5:11** And not only *so*, but we also joy in God through our Lord Jesus Christ, by whom we have now received **the atonement.**

We are saved from the wrath of God's judgment through faith in God's Son being justified/made righteous by his blood. We have been made righteous because Christ bore our iniquities and shed his blood in exchange for our souls. Jesus conquered sin for us by being obedient unto death, and then he conquered death and rose the third day. Death could not hold him without sin's grip (Php 2:8; Act 2:24). Reconciled to God by his death we are delivered daily by him as he lives his resurrection life in us (Gal 2:20).

> **Rom 5:19** For as by one man's disobedience many were made sinners, so by the obedience of one shall many be made righteous.

THE EXCHANGE / RECONCILIATION

2Co 5:17 Therefore if any man be in Christ, he is a new creature: old things are passed away; behold, all things are become new.

2Co 5:18 And all things are of God, who hath **reconciled us to himself** by Jesus Christ, and hath given to us the ministry of reconciliation;

2Co 5:19 To wit, that God was in Christ, reconciling the world unto himself, **not imputing their trespasses** unto them; and hath committed unto us the word of reconciliation.

2Co 5:20 Now then we are ambassadors for Christ, as though God did beseech you by us: we pray you in Christ's stead, **be ye reconciled to God.**

2Co 5:21 For he hath **made him** *to be* **sin for us**, who knew no sin; that we might be **made the righteousness of God** in him.

- imputing—taking inventory of, accounting, esteeming, reckoning.

We have received this atonement, this great exchange of his righteousness for our sins if we have believed in Jesus who gave himself for us. All of us were astray from God going our own way, but God's Son, the lamb of God, provided forgiveness and restoration by laying on him all our iniquity. Sins are not imputed to those who believe in Christ Jesus, for all judgment of sin was put on him. For those who look to the Holy One who bore our cross, there is salvation.

Isa 53:3 He is despised and rejected of men; a man of sorrows, and acquainted with grief: and we hid as it were *our* faces from him; he was despised, and we esteemed him not.

Isa 53:4 Surely he hath borne our griefs, and carried our sorrows: yet we did esteem him stricken, smitten of God, and afflicted.

Isa 53:5 But he *was* wounded for our transgressions, *he was* bruised for our iniquities: the chastisement of our peace *was* upon him; and with his stripes we are healed.

Isa 53:6 All we like sheep have gone astray; we have turned every one to his own way; and the LORD hath **laid on him the iniquity of us all.**

Isa 53:7 He was oppressed, and he was afflicted, yet he opened not his mouth: **he is brought as a lamb to the slaughter**, and as a sheep before her shearers is dumb, so he openeth not his mouth.

Isa 53:8 He was taken from prison and from judgment: and **who shall declare his generation?** for he was cut off out of the land of the living: for the transgression of my people was he stricken.

Isa 53:9 And he made his grave with the wicked, and with the rich in his death; because he had done no violence, neither *was any* deceit in his mouth.

Isa 53:10 Yet it pleased the LORD to bruise him; he hath put *him* to grief: when thou shalt make **his soul an offering for sin**...

Isa 53:11   He shall see of the travail of his soul, *and* shall be satisfied: **by his knowledge** shall my righteous servant justify many; for he shall bear their iniquities.

The life of the flesh is in the blood, and only the life with pure and holy blood can atone for the soul of man. Christ's body and blood was the offering, the sacrificial lamb to take away the sins of the world. The blood of bulls and goats could never put away sins, but the blood of Jesus did. He destroyed its power over us by his knowledge (Isa 53). If the princes of this world (devils) had known that by killing the Prince of Peace they were sealing their fate, they would not have done it (1Co 2). But God who alone has all knowledge and wisdom outsmarted the devil. The devil thought he was victorious over the seed of the woman (Gen 3:16). Instead, Satan's plan backfired, and he was the recipient of a fatal blow. When Jesus rose from the dead, it was a mighty triumph over Satan.

When we believe in Jesus as Lord and Savior, we are washed in the blood, raised from the dead, made righteous, reconciled to God. We become a new man with a new life. He put his Spirit in us, and we no longer walk the path of the wicked. Instead of the spirit of disobedience, we have within the obedient Christ, the Holy One.

Eph 2:1   And **you** *hath he quickened,* **who were dead** in trespasses and sins;

Eph 2:2   Wherein in time past ye walked according to the course of this world, according to the prince of the power of the air, the spirit that now worketh in the children of disobedience:

REDEMPTION THROUGH HIS BLOOD-RANSOMED

- redemption: ransom in full, deliverance.

Eph 1:7 In whom we have **redemption through his blood, the forgiveness of sins,** according to the riches of his grace;

Heb 9:11 Neither by the blood of goats and calves, but **by his own blood** he entered in once into the **holy place,** having obtained **eternal redemption** *for us.*

1Co 6:19 What? know ye not that your body is the temple of the Holy Ghost *which is* in you, which ye have of God, and **ye are not your own?**

1Co 6:20 For **ye are bought with a price**: therefore glorify God in your body, and in your spirit, which are God's.

Jesus holy body and blood was the ransom price for the exchange that we might be reconciled to God. We do not belong to ourselves now but to him who bought us with his blood. His life for ours so we could be forgiven and have eternal life through his death and resurrection.

RESTORATION OF A PURE CONSCIENCE

Before Adam and Eve sinned their conscience was pure: they were only conscious or aware of God's goodness. Man's conscience became defiled by sin through the disobedience of Adam which resulted in death. Eve was deceived by the serpent, but Adam was not. He was aware (his conscience knew) that he was doing wrong in disobeying God (1 Tim 2:14). Adam's sin was willful.

After their experience with sin, they became conscious they were naked because there was an immediate change, a death. Sin had entered and defiled their conscience. They lost the covering of their righteousness, and they sought to cover themselves by making coverings of leaves. The works of man, however clever, are not the solution to take away sin nor its consequences. He cannot restore the purity of his conscience nor his body. The scripture says that God saw that there was no man, no intercessor, so he sent his right arm to save: his Son (Isa 59:16).

Through Christ is restoration. He purges our conscience from the dead works of sin and resurrects our spirit man. Now we are clothed with Christ righteousness which has been imputed to us by faith. Next, we are to be renewed in the attitude of our mind until lastly our mind and body shall be presented holy and blameless; glorified at the resurrection (1Co 15).

> **Heb 9:13** For if the blood of bulls and of goats, and the ashes of an heifer sprinkling the unclean, sanctifieth to the purifying of the flesh:
>
> **Heb 9:14** How much more shall the **blood of Christ**, who through the eternal Spirit offered himself without spot to God, **purge your conscience from dead works** to serve the living God?
>
> **Heb 10:4** For *it is* not possible that the blood of bulls and of goats should take away sins.
>
> **Heb 10:5** Wherefore when **he cometh into the world**, he saith, Sacrifice and offering thou wouldest not, but **a body hast thou prepared me**:
>
> **Heb 10:6** In burnt offerings and *sacrifices* for sin thou hast had no pleasure.
>
> **Heb 10:7** Then said I, **Lo, I come** (in the volume of the book it is written of me,) **to do thy will, O God.**

Our Redeemer came to take away and deliver us from the power of sin and death. A holy and pure man's body was needed to destroy the body of sin, and his blood was needed to purge man's conscience from the working of death. Jesus came from above to do his Father's will, and because he was faithful to fulfill his mission we have been made free from sin and death. Instead of death working in the conscience, the believer now has God's life working in the conscience. We are made righteous and empowered by his Holy Spirit. When we hear and believe the truth of the gospel, the seed of Christ becomes planted in our hearts, and the body of sin is destroyed in us because Christ dwells in us and we in him. The blood he shed to make an atonement for sins ratifies the New Covenant within us, and our conscience is purged (Rom. 6:6). Jesus body was resurrected in glory, and we are alive in him. Since we are a new creation of his making, let us follow after that for which we were ordained (Eph 2:10). It is God's will.

BORN AGAIN OF THE SPIRIT

Joh 3:1   There was a man of the Pharisees, named Nicodemus, a ruler of the Jews:

Joh 3:2   The same came to Jesus by night, and said unto him, Rabbi, we know that thou art a teacher come from God: for no man can do these miracles that thou doest, except God be with him.

Joh 3:3   Jesus answered and said unto him, Verily, verily, I say unto thee, Except a man be **born again,** he cannot see the kingdom of God.

Joh 3:4   Nicodemus saith unto him, How can a man be born when he is old? can he enter the second time into his mother's womb, and be born?

Joh 3:5   Jesus answered, Verily, verily, I say unto thee, Except a man be **born of water and *of* the Spirit,** he cannot enter into the kingdom of God.

Joh 3:6 That which is born of the flesh is flesh; and that which is born of the Spirit is spirit.

- That which is born of the Spirit is spirit.

Joh 6:63 It is the spirit that quickeneth; the flesh profiteth nothing: **the words that I speak unto you, *they* are spirit, and *they* are life.**

1Pe 1:23 Being born again, not of corruptible seed, but of **incorruptible, by the word of God,** which liveth and abideth for ever.

BORN OF INCORRUPTIBLE SEED

When Jesus said you must be born again of the water and the spirit, he was speaking of the washing of the water of the incorruptible word of God and the working of the Holy Spirit of God in us to renew.

2Co 5:17 Therefore if any man *be* in Christ, *he is* a new creature: old things are passed away; behold, all things are become new.

The washing of regeneration and renewing of the Holy Ghost Paul spoke of in Titus makes us new creations in Christ Jesus. The nature of the first Adam in us has passed away, and now we have a new life with different desires; those that lead to righteousness because in him we have been made righteous. Whoever is born of God does not practice sin because he has a new nature. It is this new creation that cannot sin for the seed of Christ remains within.

The Son of God was manifested to destroy the works of sin. The mind and body, however are not spiritual and must be renewed to the image of the Christ within who cannot sin.

1 Jn 3:8 He that committeth sin is of the devil; for the devil sinneth from the beginning. For this purpose **the Son of God was manifested, that he might destroy the works of the devil.**

1 Jn 3:9 Whosoever is born of God doth not commit sin; **for his seed remaineth in him: and he cannot sin, because he is born of God.**

In Genesis, we find the foundation for understanding who God is and man and God's purpose for him. God is the originator of all that exists, and he planned and created an environment for man's benefit. Man is not an animal but an intricate human being designed by God to fellowship with God. He was shaped and molded by the hands of the Almighty himself into his image and given life when God breathed his breath into him. When Adam sinned, the whole human race was brought down to a level of knowing good and evil, and the entire world was defiled under its sway. Adam and Eve had only known good up to that point. God chose to cover man sins until the promised seed should come that could contain the pure and holy properties needed to transform all of humanity. Unlike Adam, the seed of Jesus is incorruptible because he is the Son of God who cannot sin. Therefore his seed will remain in those born again for we partake of his immortal and incorruptible nature through his word (2 Pet 1:3-4).

The sacrifice of the soul of The Savior would be the only atonement to pay for all sin and guilt, yet enough to regenerate all humanity throughout all ages. Those who are born again are born as pure new creations in spirit.

God's plan for man has always been for good, and we should be humbled and grateful for his graciousness toward us. Knowing that our Creator desires a relationship with each of us whom he considers beloved should fill us with awe and inspire us to draw near to understand him better.

SALVATION ONLY IN JESUS NAME

1Co 6:11 And such were some of you: but ye are washed, but ye are sanctified, but ye are justified **in the name of the Lord Jesus**, and by the Spirit of our God.

- washed—(wash fully, have remitted) remitted—forgiven.

- sanctified—(make holy, purify, consecrate).

- justified—(to render just or innocent, to free, be righteous).

The preaching of the cross, which is foolishness to the world is the power of God that brings salvation. The Atonement which washed our sins away and bought our salvation is a gift that is received through faith when we hear the good news of the gospel and call on Jesus name. When we believe in Christ's work of atonement on the cross and call on Christ for salvation, we are washed, sanctified and justified in the name of Jesus. There is no other name we can call on for his name is exalted above every name.

Php 2:8 And being found in fashion as a man, he humbled himself, and became obedient unto death, even the death of the cross.

Php 2:9 Wherefore God also hath highly exalted him, and given him a **name which is above every name:**

Php 2:10 That at the name of Jesus every knee should bow, of *things* in heaven, and *things* in earth, and *things* under the earth;

Php 2:11 And *that* every tongue should **confess** that **Jesus Christ *is* Lord**, to the glory of God the Father.

Act 2:21   And it shall come to pass, *that* whosoever shall call on **the name of the Lord** shall be saved.

Act 4:12   Neither is there salvation in any other: for there is **none other name** under heaven given among men, whereby we must be saved.

Rom 10:9   That if thou shalt **confess with thy mouth the Lord Jesus,** and shalt **believe in thine heart** that God hath raised him from the dead, thou shalt be saved.

Rom 10:10   For with the heart man believeth unto righteousness; and with the mouth confession is made unto salvation.

Rom 10:11   For the scripture saith, Whosoever believeth on him shall not be ashamed.

Calling on Jesus name, confessing him as Lord (master) and believing with all your heart that God raised him from the dead will result in being saved. Christ Jesus is our wisdom, our righteousness, our sanctification and our redemption. His name is above every name in heaven and in earth and to Jesus everyone who has ever lived will bow.

In the name of Jesus Christ the Lord the Apostles worked miracles and preached the Gospel of the Kingdom of God, the Gospel of Peace.

LESSON 2

Doctrine of Baptisms

OBJECTIVE: Develop and demonstrate an understanding of baptisms.

BAPTISM WITH WATER

The history of baptism has its roots in the Jewish rites of purification as directed in the books of Moses. The purification waters were for the cleansing from various uncleannesses i.e., touching a corpse, leper, and other multiple defilements. The rite was extended to include purification for Gentile converts as long as they were circumcised too. The pool of Siloam where Jesus sent the blind man to wash is said to be a Jewish Ritual Bath called a Mikveh. Also, the pool of Bethesda with its five porches is thought to be a Mikveh (Joh 5:1-8). After the birth of Jesus, Mary went through a time of purification. After going to the Mikveh, she could enter the temple of the Lord (Lk 2:22).

In contrast to the sanctification of the purification waters according to the law, John baptized in the Jordan River. John the Baptist was the son of Zechariah the Priest, his birth a miracle like that of Isaac. He was destined to be the forerunner of the Lord to declare his Coming. He would be the witness when Messiah appeared that he was the Lamb of God who takes away the sins of the world. For this reason, he came baptizing.

> Mat 3:1 In those days came John the Baptist, preaching in the wilderness of Judaea.
>
> Mat 3:2 And saying, Repent ye: for the kingdom of heaven is at hand.
>
> Mat 4:3 For this is he that was spoken of by the prophet Esaias, saying, **The voice of one crying in the wilderness, Prepare ye the way of the Lord**, make his paths straight.

John was the voice of one crying in the wilderness, make ready the way of the Lord (Isa 40:3).

He preached repentance and baptized with water but declared that the one coming after him, the Christ, would baptize with the Holy Ghost and Fire. When John saw Jesus coming to his baptism, he witnessed to the crowd that Jesus was the one he had been speaking of who was preferred before him because he was before him. He knew by the Spirit that it was Jesus who would baptize with the Holy Ghost and fire.

> Joh 1:29 The next day John seeth Jesus coming unto him, and saith, Behold the Lamb of God, which taketh away the sin of the world.
>
> Joh 1:30 This is he of whom I said, After me cometh a man which is preferred before me: for **he was before me.**
>
> Joh 1:31 **And I knew him not**: but that he should be **made manifest to Israel, therefore am I come baptizing with water.**

Joh 1:32 And John bare record, saying, I saw the Spirit descending from heaven like a dove, and it abode upon him.

Joh 1:33 And **I knew him not**: but he that sent me to baptize with water, the same said unto me, Upon whom thou shalt see the Spirit descending, and remaining on him, the same is he which baptizeth with the Holy Ghost.

Joh 1:34 And I saw, and bare record that this is the Son of God.

John, in saying that he was after him yet before him was revealing that he believed Jesus to be the Son of God sent from above the Everlasting One, the Redeemer, the Holy One (Isa 48:12-17; Mic 5:1-2 Isa 53). When he saw Jesus, God revealed to him that this was The Holy One, the Lamb of God! It was shown to him by the Father in a vision whereby he saw a dove descending upon Jesus. Oh, how he must have thought about and yearned for the day that Jesus could baptize him with the Holy Spirit. Then the day came that Christ came out to be baptized by John. John instead wanted Jesus to baptize him. Jesus replied that he wanted to fulfill all righteousness and so he was baptized.

When he came up from the waters of John's baptism, the Holy Spirit descended like a dove, and the Father spoke from heaven proclaiming that this was his beloved son and that he was well pleased with him. Here we see the Trinity revealed. The Holy Spirit who descended and the Father who spoke from Heaven are they who sent the Son (Isa 48:12-17).

Mat 3:11 I indeed baptize you with water unto repentance: but he that cometh after me is mightier than I, whose shoes I am not worthy to bear: he shall baptize you with the Holy Ghost, and *with* fire:

Mat 3:12 Whose fan *is* in his hand, and he will throughly purge his floor, and gather his wheat into the garner; but he will **burn up the chaff** with unquenchable fire.

Mat 3:13 Then cometh Jesus from Galilee to Jordan unto John, to be baptized of him.

Mat 3:14 But John forbad him, saying, I have need to be baptized of thee, and comest thou to me?

Mat 3:15 And Jesus answering said unto him, Suffer *it to be so* now: for thus it becometh us to fulfil all righteousness. Then he suffered him.

Mat 3:16 And Jesus, when he was baptized, went up straightway out of the water: and, lo, the heavens were opened unto him, and **he saw the Spirit of God descending like a dove, and lighting upon him:**

Mat 3:17 And lo **a voice from heaven, saying, This is my beloved Son,** in whom I am well pleased.

It was time for Christ to manifest himself to Israel, so John came baptizing in obedience to God's command. Jesus was baptized to fulfill all righteousness. He was identifying with us although he had no sin consciousness of his own. That is why his Father could say this is my son in whom I am well pleased. Later when asked a question of the Pharisees regarding who gave him authority, Jesus asked them if they believed the baptism of John was from heaven or of men. He was saying that his authorization was from the same source as John's, the Father. So we see that water baptism was from God and not man. After Christ began to minister, he authorized his disciples to baptize in water also, though Christ himself baptized no one.

Joh 4:1   When therefore the Lord knew how the Pharisees had heard that **Jesus made and baptized more disciples than John.**

Joh 4:2   (Though **Jesus himself baptized not**, but his disciples,)

Joh 4:3   He left Judaea, and departed again into Galilee.

Mat 21:23   And when he was come into the temple, the chief priests and the elders of the people came unto him as he was teaching, and said, By what authority doest thou these things? and who gave thee this authority?

Mat 21:24   And Jesus answered and said unto them, I also will ask you one thing, which if ye tell me, I in like wise will tell you by what authority I do these things.

Mat 21:25   The baptism of John, whence was it? **from heaven, or of men?** And they reasoned with themselves, saying, If we shall say, From heaven; he will say unto us, Why did ye not then believe him?

■ John baptized with water that Jesus would be made manifest to Israel.

BAPTISM INTO CHRIST

- baptism—to make whelmed, to fully wet.

- whelm—to engulf, submerge, **BURY** (someone or something).

Rom 6:3 Know ye not, that so many of **us as were baptized into Jesus Christ were baptized into his death?**

Rom 6:4 Therefore we are **buried with him by baptism into death:** that like as Christ was raised up from the dead by the glory of the Father, even so we also should walk in newness of life.

Rom 6:5 For if we have been planted together in the likeness of his death, we shall be also *in the likeness* of *his* resurrection:

Rom 6:6 Knowing this, that **our old man is crucified with** *him*, **that the body of sin might be destroyed,** that henceforth **we should not serve sin.**

One of the meanings of baptism is to bury. We are crucified with Christ Jesus, and our body is dead and buried with him because of sin. However, our spirit is alive because of the righteousness that Christ imputed to us. We have put him on, and he lives in us. We are called to live this new life in him, and we shall obtain the promise of his resurrection.

BAPTIZED INTO HIS DEATH ROM 6:3-6

- Crucified with Christ Gal. 2:20.

- Body is dead Ro 8:10.

- Buried with him by baptism into his death.

- Raised with him in new life.

Gal 2:20   **I am crucified with Christ**: nevertheless I live; yet not I, but **Christ liveth in me:** and the life which I now live in the flesh I live by the faith of the Son of God, who loved me, and gave himself for me.

ONE BODY & ONE SPIRIT–OUR JOINING

1Co 12:13   For **by one Spirit** are we all **baptized into one body,** whether *we be* Jews or Gentiles, whether *we be* bond or free; and have been **all made to drink into one Spirit.**

1Co 6:17   But he that is **joined unto the Lord is one spirit.**

Eph 1:22   And hath put all *things* under his feet, and gave him *to be* the **head** over all *things* to **the church.**

Eph 1: 23   Which is his body, the fulness of him that filleth all in all.

Eph 2:5   Even when we were dead in sins, hath **quickened us together with Christ,** (by grace ye are saved;)

Eph 2:6   And hath raised *us* up together, and made *us* sit together in heavenly *places* in Christ Jesus:

We are transformed into New Creations baptized by the Holy Spirit and joined in body and Spirit. Old things have passed away; the old man is dead with Christ. Christ put our sins away, and all things became new because we are raised with him in the power of his Resurrection; made alive to God through Jesus Christ. God desires that we walk in the light of that newness of life in loving fellowship with him and with one another in the oneness of Spirit.

Eph 4:4   *There is* **one body, and one Spirit**, even as ye are called in one hope of your calling;

Eph 4:5   One Lord, one faith, **one baptism.**

Baptism into Christ is the baptism that saves and that is why the scripture says there is one baptism.

BAPTISM IN THE NAME OF THE FATHER, SON & HOLY GHOST

We are commissioned by the Lord to baptize with water even as John the Baptist was commissioned by God. John baptized that Jesus might be manifested to Israel. Being commissioned by Jesus, we therefore baptize that Jesus might be manifested to the world.

Mat 28:18   And Jesus came and spake unto them, saying, All power is given unto me in heaven and in earth.

Mat 28:19   Go ye therefore, and **teach all nations, baptizing them in the name of the Father, and of the Son, and of the Holy Ghost:**

Mat 28:20   Teaching them to observe all things whatsoever I have commanded you: and, lo, I am with you alway, *even* unto the end of the world. Amen.

Jesus is the fullness of the Godhead in his body. The Father and the Holy Spirit dwell in him, and it is through Jesus that we are in the Father and the Spirit. The self-existent, eternal one was made known under the Old Covenant to the nation of Israel by the name Jehovah. Jehovah was the Jewish national name of God. He is known as Jesus (Jehoshua), God, is my Salvation in the New Covenant. Both The Father and The Son are called LORD.

Jesus, the Lord is speaking in (Isa 48) as the one sent from the Lord God and his Spirit. When Jesus prayed in (John 17), he said that he had manifested the Father's name and asked the Father to return to him the glory that he shared with the Father before. Jesus commanded the disciples to baptize in the name of the Father, Son, and Holy Spirit. In (Act 10) Peter commanded they be baptized in the name of the Lord and in (Act 8) Phillip baptized in the name of Jesus. There is no contradiction. The scripture states that God has exalted the name of Jesus above every name in heaven and earth and all shall bow and confess him as Lord. By inheritance, Jesus has obtained a more excellent name than the angels (Heb 1). He inherited his Father's name of course. The Father was in Christ reconciling the world to himself. They shared the same name in the Old Covenant, and they share the same in the new, and they share the glory in the Godhead. Jehovah, the Redeemer, was sent by Jehovah the Father and Holy Spirit. GOD is truly our salvation.

> **Isa 48:16** Come ye near unto me, hear ye this; I have not spoken in secret from the beginning; from the time that it was, there *am* I: and now **the Lord GOD, and his Spirit, hath sent me.**
>
> **Isa 48:17** Thus saith the **LORD (Jehovah), thy Redeemer, the Holy One of Israel;** I *am* the **LORD (Jehovah) thy God** which teacheth thee to profit, which leadeth thee by the way *that* thou shouldest go.
>
> Act 10:44 While Peter yet spake these words, **the Holy Ghost fell** on all them which heard the word.
>
> Act 10:45 And they of the circumcision which believed were astonished, as many as came with Peter, because that on the Gentiles also was **poured out the gift of the Holy Ghost.**

Act 10:46 For they heard them speak with tongues, and magnify God. Then answered Peter.

Act 10:47 Can any man forbid water, that these should not be baptized, **which have received the Holy Ghost as well as we?**

Act 10:48 And **he commanded them to be baptized in the name of the Lord.** Then prayed they him to tarry certain days.

Act 8:16 (For as yet he was fallen upon none of them: only they were **baptized in the name of the Lord Jesus.**)

As Paul was passing through Ephesus, he found some disciples of John. He asked them if they had received the Holy Ghost (Spirit) since they believed and they had not even heard about the baptism of the Holy Ghost. Perhaps they were baptized by one of John's disciples. Paul baptizes them again in the name of Jesus, and then he laid hands on them, and they received the Holy Ghost and spoke with tongues and prophesied (Act 19:1-6).

- Jesus disciples baptized with water that Jesus might be manifested to the World.

WATER BAPTISM IS A FIGURE OF OUR BAPTISM INTO CHRIST JESUS

1Pe 3:20 Which sometime were disobedient, when once the long-suffering of God waited in the days of Noah, while the ark was a preparing, wherein few, that is, eight souls were **saved by water.**

1Pe 3:21 The **like figure** whereunto *even* baptism doth also now save us (not the putting away of the filth of the flesh, but the answer of a good conscience toward God) by the resurrection of Jesus Christ:

- conscience—our co-perception, our moral consciousness.

Peter here is referring to water baptism being a figure (picture, symbol) of the baptism which cleanses the conscience. Water can only wash the flesh. Through faith in Christ, we are baptized into his death and resurrection by the power of the Holy Spirit. Our conscience has been purged of dead works and is now aware of righteousness instead of sin. Water baptism cannot save but presents a picture of our baptism into Christ death, burial and resurrection. Through faith in Jesus, we have a new life in him and have been made righteous.

> **Heb 9:13** How much more shall the blood of Christ, who through the eternal Spirit offered himself without spot to God, **purge your conscience from dead works** to serve the living God?

> **Rom 10:8** But what saith it? The word is nigh thee, even in thy mouth, and in thy heart: that is, **the word of faith, which we preach**;

> **Rom 10:9** That if thou shalt confess with thy mouth the Lord Jesus, and shalt believe in thine heart that God hath raised him from the dead, thou shalt be saved.

> **Rom 10:10** For with the heart man believeth unto righteousness; and with the mouth confession is made unto salvation.

When Philip preached to the Eunuch, he told him that he must believe with all his heart before he would baptize him in water. In other words, he must understand the preaching of the cross of

Christ believe in his resurrection with all his heart and confess Jesus is Lord for salvation. After that Philip would agree to baptize him. The emphasis is what takes place within the heart of man: faith. Whosoever believes in the Son of God will not perish but have everlasting life.

It is our faith in Christ Jesus that causes us to follow him in water baptism. Jesus knew the water baptism did not make him holy but was to fulfill all righteousness and for a witness to the people. We are baptized in water to follow his example, to be obedient to declare his righteousness to the world.

> Act 8:36 And as they went on *their* way, they came unto a certain water: and the eunuch said, See, *here is* water; **what doth hinder me to be baptized?**
>
> Act 8:37 And Philip said, **If thou believest with all thine heart,** thou mayest. And he answered and said, I believe that Jesus Christ is the Son of God.
>
> Act 8:38 And he commanded the chariot to stand still: and they went down both into the water, both Philip and the eunuch; and he baptized him.

Paul makes it clear what saves. The people of Corinth put much stock in whom they were baptized by to the extent that they argued amongst themselves. Paul put the emphasis back where it needed to be, not on baptism in water but the preaching of the cross of Jesus Christ which had the power to save.

> 1Co 1:17 For **Christ sent me not to baptize, but to preach the gospel:** not with wisdom of words, lest the cross of Christ should be made of none effect.
>
> 1Co 1:18 For **the preaching of the cross** is to them that perish foolishness; but unto us which are saved **it is the power of God.**

BAPTISM WITH THE HOLY GHOST & FIRE

Mat 3:11 I indeed baptize you with water unto repentance: but he that cometh after me is mightier than I, whose shoes I am not worthy to bear: **he shall baptize you with the Holy Ghost, and** *with* **fire:**

Mat 3:12 Whose fan *is* in his hand, and **he will throughly purge his floor,** and gather his wheat into the garner; but he will burn up the chaff with unquenchable fire.

POWER TO WITNESS

Act 1:8 **But ye shall receive power, after that the Holy Ghost is come upon you: and ye shall be witnesses** unto me both in Jerusalem, and in all Judaea, and in Samaria, and unto the uttermost part of the earth.

Pentecost is a Jewish feast celebrating the spring harvest. It is believed to be when Moses received the law from God on Mt. Sinai and brought it down to the people. They had agreed to obey God's commandments and entered into a covenant with him. God descended upon the Mount in fire and Moses went up to receive the tablets. The people fell back into idolatry while Moses was on the Mount receiving the tablets of the law. When Moses returned and found the people worshipping an idol, he threw the stone tablets down and broke them. That day 3000 people died from God's wrath because they worshiped the golden calf breaking his commandments. According to (2Co 3) the law was a ministration of death, but the new covenant is a ministration of the Spirit.

Joh 1:17 For the law was given by Moses, *but* grace and truth came by Jesus Christ.

Joh 1:18 No man hath seen God at any time; the only begotten Son, which is in the bosom of the Father, **he hath declared** *him.*

On the day of Pentecost Jesus received from his Father, the Spirit of Grace which he poured out upon his disciples on Mt. Zion in Jerusalem, and 3000 souls were saved. God descended in fire on Mt. Sinai when the law was given (Exo 19:18). The Holy Spirit descended as a mighty rushing wind accompanied by tongues of fire. That was the beginning of what many call the Dispensation of Grace or the Church Age. The souls that received the Holy Spirit that day became the first fruits of the Harvest, in fulfillment of the promise of the Feast of Pentecost. As the feasts of Passover and Unleavened Bread were fulfilled in our Lord and Savior's first coming, the feast of Pentecost saw its fulfillment in the outpouring of the Holy Spirit.

Act 2:1 And when the **day of Pentecost** was fully come, they were all with one accord in one place.

Act 2:2 And suddenly there came a sound from heaven as of a rushing mighty wind, and it filled all the house where they were sitting.

Act 2:3 And there appeared unto them cloven tongues like as of fire, and it sat upon each of them.

Act 2:4 And they were **all filled with the Holy Ghost,** and began to speak with other tongues, as the Spirit gave them utterance.

The power to witness is what Jesus was speaking of In (Joh 15) when he said the Holy Spirit would testify of him. The Holy Spirit testifies through men and women in a demonstration of power. After the disciples were baptized in the Holy Spirit, they bore witness of the Resurrection of Jesus with great power. Jesus said signs would follow those who believe and in his name they would do mighty works of God (Mar 16). Those works are a witness of Jesus resurrection and can only be accomplished with the power of the Holy Spirit. After the day of Pentecost Peter and John were entering the temple and there was a man crippled from birth who was begging alms. Peter, having nothing to give in the natural, gave him what he had in the Spirit; the power and authority of Jesus name to heal.

Act 3:6   Then Peter said, Silver and gold have I none; but **such as I have give I thee: In the name of Jesus Christ of Nazareth** rise up and walk.

Act 4:33   And **with great power gave the apostles witness of the resurrection** of the Lord Jesus: and great grace was upon them all.

1Co 2:4   And my speech and my preaching *was* not with enticing words of man's wisdom, but **in demonstration of the Spirit and of power:**

TONGUES AS OF FIRE

Mar 16:17   And these **signs shall follow them that believe; In my name** shall they cast out devils; they **shall speak with new tongues;**

Mar 16:18   They shall take up serpents; and if they drink any deadly thing, it shall not hurt them; they shall lay hands on the sick, and they shall recover.

Act 2:3   And there appeared unto them **cloven tongues like as of fire,** and it sat upon each of them.

Act 2:4   And they were all **filled with the Holy Ghost, and began to speak with other tongues, as the Spirit gave them utterance.**

- cloven—to partition in distribution, to divide.
- tongues—a language naturally not acquired.

Act 2:11   Cretes and Arabians, we do hear them **speak in our tongues** the wonderful works of God.

Act 2:16   But this is that which was spoken by the prophet Joel;

Act 2:17   And it shall come to pass in the last days, saith God, **I will pour out of my Spirit upon all flesh: and your sons and your daughters shall prophesy,** and your young men shall see visions, and your old men shall dream dreams:

Act 2:18   And on my servants and on my handmaidens I will pour out in those days of my Spirit; and **they shall prophesy:**

- prophesy— to foretell events, divine, speak under inspiration, exercise a prophetic office.

Joe 2:28   And it shall come to pass afterward, *that* **I will pour out my spirit upon all flesh; and your sons and your daughters shall prophesy,** your old men shall dream dreams, your young men shall see visions:

Joe 2:29 And also upon the servants and upon the handmaids in those days will I pour out my spirit.

Joe 2:30 And I will shew wonders in the heavens and in the earth, blood, and fire, and pillars of smoke.

Joe 2:31 The sun shall be turned into darkness, and the moon into blood, **before the great and the terrible day of the LORD come.**

God promised through the prophet Joel that he would pour out his Spirit upon all flesh. When the day came, it was no small stir. Many heard the sound of the mighty rushing wind of the Spirit and ran to the scene. They listened to the disciples speaking in tongues the glorious works of God in the languages of their nations. Although those from other countries understood those who spoke in tongues, they could not distinguish themselves unless one interpreted. Then Peter with great power stood and expouned on the event and preached the gospel. About three thousand souls were added to the church that day. Since then millions have confessed Jesus as Lord, many at the cost of their lives.

Act 2:32 This Jesus hath God raised up, whereof we all are **witnesses.**

Act 2:33 Therefore being by the right hand of God exalted, and having received of the Father **the promise of the Holy Ghost,** he hath shed forth this, which ye now see and hear.

Luk 11:13 If ye then, being evil, know how to give good gifts unto your children: how much more shall *your* heavenly Father give the **Holy Spirit to them that ask him**?

The devil has tried very hard to keep the life of Jesus from being manifested in the children of God. He has caused people to be afraid of the gift of the Spirit because he knows the Holy Spirit will help direct their lives to serve God in a supernatural way instead of natural. The promise of the Holy Spirit is what our Lord Jesus has poured out. We do not have to fear what God has given. If we ask for the Holy Spirit, we will not receive a stone or a serpent. God has provided a way to pray that can surpass our understanding and when we pray in the Holy Ghost, we are building up ourselves spiritually in the faith (Jud 1:20). Paul says I will pray with the understanding and I will pray with the Spirit. He instructs us to pray that we may interpret that our minds may also be fruitful (1 Co 14).

BAPTISM OF THE FIRES OF JUDGMENT

Mat 3:5   Then went out to him Jerusalem, and all Judaea, and all the region round about Jordan.

Mat 3:6   And were baptized of him in Jordan, confessing their sins.

Mat 3:7   But when he saw many of the Pharisees and Sadducees come to his baptism, he said unto them, O generation of vipers, who hath warned you to flee from the **wrath to come?**

Mat 3:8   Bring forth therefore fruits meet for repentance:

Mat 3:9   And think not to say within yourselves, We have Abraham to *our* father: for I say unto you, that God is able of these stones to raise up children unto Abraham.

Mat 3:10 And now also the axe is laid unto the root of the trees: therefore every tree which bringeth not forth good fruit is hewn down, and **cast into the fire.**

Mat 3:11 I indeed baptize you with water unto repentance: but he that cometh after me is mightier than I, whose shoes I am not worthy to bear: **he shall baptize you with the Holy Ghost, and *with* fire:**

Mat 3:12 Whose fan *is* in his hand, and he will throughly purge his floor, and gather his **wheat** into the garner; but he will **burn up the chaff with unquenchable fire.**

John the Baptist was speaking to a mixed company from all the region around and many Pharisees and Sadducees also. Some were genuinely repentant of their sins, probably a few just curious, and some like the religious leaders come only to watch and report back to the chief priests. John, knowing their self-righteousness gave them a stern warning about trusting in the wrong thing, like their heritage as children of Abraham. He makes it clear that all men should bring forth fruit that true repentance produces. The trees that do not bear fruit are cut down and burned in the fire. The chaff is removed from the grain and cast into the flame also, but the grain is gathered and stored in the barn. John gave these two examples to demonstrate that the baptism in fire is judgment for the wicked but a purifier of the righteous. The wicked will be separated from the saints and cast into everlasting unquenchable fire, but the righteous taken from the earth to their new home. Unbelievers are condemned to suffer the torment of hell with the god of this world who has been judged and is destined for the lake of unquenchable fire in the end (Joh 16:8-11; Rev 20:15).

The wheat (saint) will have their works tried in the fire and judged, and the chaff (the flesh/world) will be burned up. Jesus gave us a parable of the good seed of the kingdom of God. He used wheat as a symbol of that good seed and tares as that seed of the enemy.

> **Mat 13:24** Another parable put he forth unto them, saying, The kingdom of heaven is likened unto a man which sowed good seed in his field:
>
> **Mat 13:25** But while men slept, his enemy came and sowed tares among the wheat, and went his way.
>
> **Mat 13:26** But when the blade was sprung up, and brought forth fruit, then appeared the tares also.
>
> **Mat 13:27** So the servants of the householder came and said unto him, Sir, didst not thou sow good seed in thy field? from whence then hath it tares?
>
> **Mat 13:28** He said unto them, An enemy hath done this. The servants said unto him, Wilt thou then that we go and gather them up?
>
> **Mat 13:29** But he said, Nay; lest while ye gather up the tares, ye root up also the wheat with them.
>
> **Mat 13:30** Let both grow together until the harvest: and in the time of harvest I will say to the reapers, Gather ye together first the tares, and bind them in bundles to burn them: but **gather the wheat into my barn.**

God sowed good seed (wheat), in his field, the world. The enemy (devil) comes and sows tares among the wheat. The tares look like the wheat until it matures and their roots become intertwined, so they are allowed to grow beside the good seed until time for the harvest. If the tares were pulled before harvest, it would uproot the wheat also. Only Jesus knows those who are his, and he shall separate and judge. Believers, portrayed as wheat, shall be harvested, purified, and gathered into Heaven, and the wicked, portrayed as tares cast in the unquenchable fire.

WORKS TRIED BY FIRE

There will be a judgment of the works of true believers and rewards will be accordingly. The fire will test all believers work, and that which are of the flesh (the chaff) will burn up like wood, hay, and stubble. Those works which are made manifest of the Spirit are of value and shall remain and will have a reward.

> **1Co 3:11** For other **foundation** can no man lay than that is laid, which is Jesus Christ.
>
> **1Co 3:12** Now if any man **build upon this foundation** gold, silver, precious stones, wood, hay, stubble;
>
> **1Co 3:13** Every man's work shall be made manifest: for the day shall declare it, because it shall be revealed by fire; and **the fire shall try every man's work** of what sort it is.
>
> **1Co 3:14** If any man's work abide which he hath built thereupon, he shall receive a reward.
>
> **1Co 3:15** If any man's work shall be burned, he shall suffer loss: but he himself shall be saved; yet so as by fire.

In the above scriptures, Paul is speaking of those who have the foundation of Christ laid in their lives. The believers work will be judged by how we build upon Christ foundation, yet even if our work burns we are saved. Salvation is a gift of God's grace, paid for by God's son. Rewards are promised for those who serve faithfully.

LESSON 3

The Holy Spirit

OBJECTIVE: Develop and demonstrate a knowledge of the Holy Spirit and his ministry.

TRIUNE GODHEAD

Many who do not believe in the triune God try to describe the Holy Spirit as just power or energy and not a person. Before Jesus was crucified, he began to teach His disciples about the Holy Spirit whom he was going to send to them after his glorification. It would be necessary for Jesus to go back to His Father that He might send the Spirit to dwell within each believer.

THE HOLY SPIRIT IS GOD

In the gospel of John chapters 14, 15, and 16 Jesus uses the pronouns 'he' and 'him' when referring to the Holy Spirit. He also uses the word 'whom' when he referred to the Holy Spirit (Joh 14:17, Joh 15:26). If the Holy Spirit is not a person, why is Jesus referring to him that way? Ananias and his wife lied to the Holy Ghost according to Peter, and he further explained that they lied to God. Jesus disciples also taught that the Holy Spirit is God. The Holy Spirit divides the gifts as he wills, so it is evident that the Holy Spirit has a mind with a will and is a Spirit being. He is self-existing with the Father and the Son as one.

> **Act 5:3** But Peter said, Ananias, why hath Satan filled thine heart to **lie to the Holy Ghost**, and to keep back *part* of the price of the land?

> **Act 5:4** Whiles it remained, was it not thine own? and after it was sold, was it not in thine own power? why hast thou conceived this thing in thine heart? **thou hast not lied unto men, but unto God.**

The scripture uses the term Godhead when referring to Father, Son, and Holy Spirit. We commonly refer to the Godhead as The Trinity because there are three persons in this Godhead.

> **Act 17:29** Forasmuch then as we are the offspring of God, we ought not to think that **the Godhead** is like unto gold, or silver, or stone, graven by art and man's device.

> **Rom 1:20** For the invisible things of him from the creation of the world are clearly seen, being understood by the things that are made, *even* **his** eternal power and **Godhead**; so that they are without excuse:

> **Col 2:8** Beware lest any man spoil you through philosophy and vain deceit, after the tradition of men, after the rudiments of the world, and not after Christ.

> **Col 2:9** For in him dwelleth all the fulness of the **Godhead** bodily.

In his letter to the Colossians Pauls states that in Christ body dwells all the fullness of the Godhead. Jesus when speaking with the disciples in John 14 told them that he would send the Holy Spirit and that he and the Father would also come and dwell within us.

The Son existed with the Father and the Spirit before he came to earth. Those who do not believe in the triune God do not accept the testimony that God sent his Son from above to become flesh. Jehovah is speaking in (Isa 48) saying Jehovah and his Spirit has sent me. Jesus is claiming to be this one sent from God and told the Pharisees that if they did not believe this, they would die in their sins. The testimony of John was that Jesus was the Word who was with God and who was God in the beginning and who became flesh. John testified that Christ came from Heaven. The Godhead from the beginning was not hidden from us. In (Gen 1) we see God creating through his Son, the Word, and the Holy Spirit who moved upon the face of the waters.

> Joh 3:31 He that cometh from above is above all: he that is of the earth is earthly, and speaketh of the earth: **he that cometh from heaven** is above all.

> Joh 8:23 And he said unto them, Ye are from beneath; **I am from above:** ye are of this world; I am not of this world.

> Joh 8:24 I said therefore unto you, that ye shall die in your sins: for if ye believe not that I am *he,* ye shall die in your sins.

When God said, "let us make man in our image," he was speaking to the Son and the Holy Spirit. God was not talking to angels because the angels did not help create anything. They are part of God's creation and are ministering spirits to the heirs of salvation (Heb 1:14).

Gen 1:1   In the beginning **God created** the heaven and the earth.

Gen 1:2   And the earth was without form, and void; and darkness *was* upon the face of the deep. And **the Spirit of God moved** upon the face of the waters.

Gen 1:3   **And God said,** Let there be light: and there was **light.**

Gen 1:26   And **God said, Let us make man** in **our image,** after **our likeness:** and let them have dominion over the fish of the sea, and over the fowl of the air, and over the cattle, and over all the earth, and over every creeping thing that creepeth upon the earth.

Joh 1:1 In the beginning was the Word, and **the Word was with God,** and **the Word was God.**

Joh 1:2   The same was in the beginning with God.

Joh 1:3   **All things were made by him;** and without him was not any thing made that was made.

Joh 1:4   In him was life; and the life was the **light of men.**

The Gospel of John chapter 1 says that all things were made by him, thus clarifying that the Word was a person by the pronoun him. Then John continues by saying that the Word became flesh and dwelt among men in verse 14. Some would argue that God cannot be triune because the scripture says the Lord our God is one Lord. In (Deu 6) the word for one in Hebrew is 'echad' and means properly united, that is one, or as an ordinal, it means first. The word 'echad' used in (Gen 2:24) is concerning husband and wife.

They become one flesh yet they are two persons. God called them Adam. The Father, Son, and Holy Spirit are one.

> **Deu 6:4** Hear, O Israel: The LORD our God *is* **one** LORD:

> **Gen 2:24** Therefore shall a man leave his father and his mother, and shall cleave unto his wife: and they shall be **one** flesh.

It is clear from these various texts that the Son of God existed before in Heaven and was The Word, the Creator. Of Jesus, the Father says, "Thy throne O God is forever and ever!" If the Father says it, that settles it!

> **Heb 1:7** And of the angels he saith, Who maketh his angels spirits, and his ministers a flame of fire.

> **Heb 1:8** But unto the Son *he saith*, **Thy throne, O God,** *is* for ever and ever: a sceptre of righteousness *is* the sceptre of thy kingdom.

SEALED WITH THE HOLY SPIRIT OF PROMISE

The Holy Spirit was sent from God the Father to dwell within us, sealing us for preservation as his own. He also is the pledge that ensures we shall receive the rest of the inheritance promised at the coming of Christ: the redemption of our bodies (Ro 8:23).

> **Eph 1:13** In whom ye also *trusted*, after that ye heard the word of truth, the gospel of your salvation: in whom also after that ye believed, **ye were sealed with that holy Spirit of promise.**

Eph 1:14 Which is **the earnest of our inheritance** until the redemption of the purchased possession, unto the praise of his glory.

- sealed—to stamp with a signet for security or preservation.
- earnest—pledge as security.

2Co 1:22 Who hath also **sealed us,** and given the **earnest of the Spirit** in our hearts.

Rom 8:11 But if the **Spirit of him that raised up Jesus from the dead** dwell in you, he that raised up Christ from the dead shall also **quicken your mortal bodies by his Spirit** that dwelleth in you.

We have received the first fruits of the Holy Spirit and long for the adoption when we receive the fullness of Christ in the last harvest (Rom 8:23). It is the same Spirit that raised Jesus from the dead that shall raise ours. When Christ returns our bodies shall be redeemed from the earth and glorified in the likeness of Christ risen body. We shall be presented before our Heavenly Father blameless; pure in spirit, soul, and body.

THE COMFORTER

Joh 14:15 If ye love me, keep my commandments.

Joh14:16 And I will pray the Father, and he shall give you **another Comforter**, that **he** may abide with you for ever;

The other Comforter is the Holy Spirit who helps with our weaknesses by making intercession for us according to the will and purpose of God. When Jesus was on earth, he interceded for his disciples and taught them. Now the Holy Spirit within each believer will be their help.

> **Rom 8:26** Likewise the Spirit also helpeth our infirmities: for we know not what we should pray for as we ought: but **the Spirit itself maketh intercession** for us with groanings which cannot be uttered.

THE SPIRIT OF TRUTH

The God of this world has blinded the minds of those who do not believe. Jesus said that we would know the truth and the truth would set us free. The Spirit of truth was with them, but He shall dwell in them. That was not possible until Christ died and rose from the dead. After Christ rose he poured out his Holy Spirit that God might tabernacle with men through the Spirit. We have become the temple of the Holy Ghost, and he will help us testify about Jesus and live the new life that is in Christ.

> **Joh 14:17** *Even* the **Spirit of truth; whom** the world cannot receive, because it seeth him not, neither knoweth him: but ye know **him;** for **he** dwelleth with you, and shall be in you.

> **Joh 14:26** But when the Comforter is come, **whom** I will send unto you from the Father, *even* **the Spirit of truth,** which proceedeth from the Father, **he shall testify of me:**

THE ANOINTING

When Jesus came out of the wilderness after forty days of fasting and prayer, he spoke this word to those in his home town of Nazareth.

> **Luk 4:18** The **Spirit of the Lord *is* upon me, because he hath anointed me** to preach the gospel to the poor; he hath sent me to heal the brokenhearted, to preach deliverance to the captives, and recovering of sight to the blind, to set at liberty them that are bruised.
>
> **Luk 4:19** To preach the acceptable year of the Lord.
>
> **Act 10:38** How God **anointed Jesus of Nazareth with the Holy Ghost and with power:** who went about doing good, and healing all that were oppressed of the devil; for God was with him.

Christ was anointed with the Holy Spirit to accomplish his ministry. Jesus was anointed with the Holy Ghost and went about doing good and healing all oppressed of the devil. We are called to do the same by the anointing of the Holy Ghost. Jesus said the works that he did we shall do also.

We have received the same Holy Spirit as Christ, and he lives in us and is our teacher. He is the Spirit of truth and will teach us all things and even as He teaches us we can live in that truth. Because the Holy Spirit is our teacher, we do not need any man to teach us. If any teach contrary to the truth of God's word, the anointing of God alerts us to the error. God has appointed teachers and preachers in the churches to train others to work in the ministry, but the Spirit shall give discernment of all teachings. The Holy Spirit who dwells within us compares spiritual with spiritual.

> **1 Jn 2:27** But **the anointing** which ye have received of him abideth in you, and ye need not that any man teach you: but as **the same anointing** teacheth you of all things, and is truth, and is no lie, and even as it hath taught you, ye shall abide in him.

- anointing—special endowment (chrism) of the Holy Spirit.

MINISTRY OF THE HOLY SPIRIT

- He Testifies of Jesus—Joh 15:26.
- He will guide us into all truth—Joh 16:13.
- He will show us things to come Joh 16:13.
- He will glorify Jesus (will show us things of Jesus)—Joh 16:14.
- He divides severally as He wills the gifts of the Spirit—1 Co 12.

Joh 15:26   But when the Comforter is come, whom I will send unto you from the Father, *even* **the Spirit of truth,** which proceedeth from the Father, **he shall testify** of me:

Joh 16:13   Howbeit when he, the **Spirit of truth, is come, he will guide you into all truth:** for he shall not speak of himself; but whatsoever he shall hear, *that* shall he speak: and **he will shew you things to come.**

Joh 16:14   **He shall glorify me:** for he shall receive of mine, and shall shew *it* unto you.

Joh 16:15   All things that the Father hath are mine: therefore said I, that **he shall take of mine, and shall shew *it* unto you.**

1Co 2:12   Now we have received, not the spirit of the world, but the spirit which is of God; **that we might know the things that are freely given to us of God.**

It is the work of the Holy Spirit to glorify Jesus and bear witness to our spirit that we are children of God. We have become heirs of God and joint heirs with Christ. If the word of Christ abides in us and we abide in him, we can ask what we will, and it will be granted (Joh 15:7). The Holy Spirit reveals to us the things of Jesus, so we will know what God's grace has freely provided for us. Once we have received a revelation of what God's grace has offered, we can ask the Father for it. The Holy Spirit will also show us things to come.

> **Rom 8:16** The Spirit itself beareth witness with our spirit, that we are the children of God:
>
> **Rom 8:17** And if children, then heirs; **heirs of God, and joint-heirs with Christ;** if so be that we suffer with *him,* that we may be also glorified together.
>
> **1Co 2:4** And **my speech and my preaching** *was* not with enticing words of man's wisdom, but **in demonstration of the Spirit and of power:**
>
> **1Co 2:5** That your faith should not stand in the wisdom of men, but in the power of God.

The Holy Spirit gives understanding and testifies by demonstrating the wisdom and power of God. We received the anointing when the Holy Spirit came that we might be Christ witnesses in all the earth. Jesus said that signs would follow those who believe. It is the Holy Spirit who is demonstrating God's power through his servants and confirming his word.

> **1Co 2:9** But as it is written, Eye hath not seen, nor ear heard, neither have entered into the heart of man, the things which God hath prepared for them that love him.
>
> **1Co 2:10 But God hath revealed** *them* **unto us by his Spirit:** for the Spirit searcheth all things, yea, the deep things of God.

1Co 2:11 For what man knoweth the things of a man, save the spirit of man which is in him? even so the things of God knoweth no man, but the Spirit of God.

1Co 2:12 Now we have received, not the spirit of the world, but the spirit which is of God; that we might know the things that are freely given to us of God.

1Co 2:13 Which things also we speak, not in the words which man's wisdom teacheth, but which the **Holy Ghost teacheth; comparing spiritual things with spiritual.**

1Co 2:14 But the natural man receiveth not the things of the Spirit of God: for they are foolishness unto him: neither can he know *them*, because they are spiritually discerned.

1Co 2:15 But **he that is spiritual judgeth all things**, yet he himself is judged of no man.

1Co 2:16 For who hath known the mind of the Lord, that he may instruct him? But **we have the mind of Christ.**

Our teacher, the Holy Spirit, gives us spiritual discernment regarding the things of God and reveals the things he has freely given us. A natural man cannot understand the spiritual because of his nature. He that is spiritual can discern spiritual matters by the wisdom of the Holy Spirit who searches the deep things of God. No one has been the Lord's counselor to instruct him, but he has given us his mind through the Spirit.

LESSON 4

Reasonable Service

OBJECTIVE: To establish an understanding of our responsibility in the transformation process.

JESUS FINISHED THE WORK OF REDEMPTION OF OUR souls on the cross. When we believe and accept Christ as our Lord, total transformation of the spirit man is complete, yet our minds and bodies are not. To address the condition of the body and mind, we are instructed to offer our bodies as a living sacrifice to God and renew our mind. We are to learn, to test, approve, examine the word, and discern by the Spirit what is God's perfect will.

Satan robs many believers of abundant life by discouraging them from even attempting to live for God. He convinces them that they cannot live righteous therefore they assume it is futile to try. One can be born again but never learn to walk in the Spirit. Our faith should not be disconnected from our responsibility to live right but should be a driving force, for the justified shall live by faith (Rom 1:17). The life and practice of a son of God reflect a trusting relationship with God that responds in faithful obedience.

It is not unreasonable for God to expect us to present ourselves to him and yield our members for his glory.

PRESENT YOUR BODIES

- reasonable—logical, ration, of the word.

Rom 12:1   I beseech you therefore, brethren, by the mercies of God, that ye **present your bodies a living sacrifice**, holy, acceptable unto God, *which is* your **reasonable service.**

Rom 12:2   And **be not conformed** to this world: but **be ye transformed** by the renewing of your mind, that ye may prove what *is* that good, and acceptable, and perfect, will of God.

When we present ourselves before God in prayer, let us yield our bodies to him and resolve (decide firmly on a course of action) to live for him.

We are alive to God through Jesus our Savior and should aspire to walk in the power of his resurrection. It begins with knowledge of Christ's victory over sin and death and how it has affected us. Because Christ has defeated sin and death these powers have no dominion over him or those baptized into his body. We are now free to serve God in this new way of life.

YIELD TO GOD

Rom 6:9   **Knowing** that Christ being raised from the dead dieth no more; **death hath no more dominion over him.**

Rom 6:10   For in that he died, he died unto sin once: but in that he liveth, he liveth unto God.

Rom 6:11   **Likewise reckon ye also yourselves to be dead indeed unto sin,** but **alive unto God through Jesus Christ our Lord.**

Rom 6:12   **Let not sin therefore reign** in your mortal body, that ye should obey it in the lusts thereof.

Rom 6:13 Neither yield ye your members *as* instruments of unrighteousness unto sin: but yield yourselves unto God, as those that are alive from the dead, and your members *as* instruments of righteousness unto God.

Rom 6:14 For **sin shall not have dominion over you:** for ye are not under the law, but under grace.

Rom 6:15   What then? shall we sin, because we are not under the law, but under grace? God forbid.

- reckon—take an inventory, estimate, **conclude,** account of, reason …

Are we accepting what the scripture claims; that we are dead to sin and alive to God and then conclude that we are?

Are we believing that we have power over sin and can reign over it?

Are we living like sin and death have no dominion over us?

We are told to consider ourselves to be dead to sin and alive to God even as Jesus is. Since we are dead to sin and alive to God, then we are conscious of God's presence without being conscious of sin. God is exhorting us not to let sin reign any longer but put off the old ways of life and walk in the new life that is in Christ. To take up the mantle of this call we have to educate ourselves with the word of God as to our new identity and purpose.

As a new creation in Christ, we have the power to bring the flesh under control. Then works of righteousness and true holiness are manifested in us instead of the old nature. God does not direct us to do something that he does not empower by the Holy Spirit.

> Rom 6:16   Know ye not, that to whom ye **yield yourselves servants to obey,** his servants ye are to whom ye obey; whether of sin unto death, or of obedience unto righteousness?
>
> Joh 8:34 Jesus answered them, Verily, verily, I say unto you, Whosoever committeth sin is the **servant of sin.**
>
> Joh 8:35   And the servant abideth not in the house for ever: *but* **the Son abideth ever.**
>
> Joh 8:36   If the Son therefore shall make you free, ye shall be free indeed.

It was Adam's disobedience to God and his obedience to Satan that brought Adam and all humanity under the dominion of sin. The evil seed of sin was planted in man and brought death upon him and all his offspring. Christ has planted good seed in those who believe imputing his righteousness to him through faith, thus bringing life. It is through God's promises that we partake of the divine nature. Becoming a son, we are no longer servants of sin, and we escape the corruption that is in the world through lusts (2 Pet 1:4; Joh 8:34-36). God expects us to yield to his command to put off the old ways and cast off the works of darkness, not making any provision for the lusts of the flesh.

> Eph 4:22   That ye **put off concerning the former conversation the old man,** which is corrupt according to the **deceitful lusts;**

Eph 4:23   And **be renewed in the spirit of your mind**;

Eph 4:24   And that ye **put on the new man,** which after God is created in righteousness and true holiness.

Rom 13:12   The night is far spent, the day is at hand: let us therefore **cast off** the **works of darkness**, and let us **put on the armour of light.**

Rom 13:13   Let us walk honestly, as in the day; not in rioting and drunkenness, not in chambering and wantonness, not in strife and envying.

Rom 13:14   But **put ye on the Lord Jesus Christ,** and **make not provision** for the flesh, to *fulfil* the lusts *thereof.*

- put off the old ways of life of the old nature which is corrupt.
- cast off works of darkness.
- do not make provision to fulfill the lusts of the flesh.
- be renewed in the spirit of your mind and put on the new man which is righteous.
- put on the armor of light.
- put on the Lord Jesus Christ.

Discover Jesus in the Word of God: Creator, Savior, King of kings and Lord of lords. The glory of his greatness and the riches of his grace and mercy are written from cover to cover. Through God's word, we arm ourselves with the armor of light which is an armor of truth. The truth of God is contrary to the darkness of the world's philosophies and is the standard by which we are to live. Putting on Christ requires the revelation of truth by the Holy Spirit.

DON'T BE CONFORMED TO THE WORLD—ROM 12:2

- conform—to fashion alike, conform to the same pattern.

Col 2:8 Beware lest any man spoil you through **philosophy and vain deceit,** after the **tradition of men, after the rudiments of the world,** and not after Christ.

The philosophy the Colossians encountered was from the Jews who wanted them to conform to the Jewish rites, i.e., circumcision. Paul explains that we who believe are circumcised in the heart and we are Jews inwardly not outwardly (Rom 2:28-29).

Even today some are trying to compel the Gentiles to keep the rites of the Jews. Whether it is after the tradition of men like the Colossians experienced or rudiments (principles) of the world, it is empty deceit, void of truth. We may not experience the same traditions of men or social influences as the Colossians but the pressure to conform to standards of today's society is enormous. In modern culture, learning institutions are prevalent that teach philosophies and traditions that are contrary to the teachings of God's word. Many deny the existence of God and the validity and infallibility in the Holy Spirit's inspiration of scriptures.

Do not conform to the pattern of the social influences of the world's philosophies: materialism, humanism, pluralism, spiritualism, and the pseudoscience of evolution.

- PHILOSOPHY—a pursuit of wisdom.

- **Materialism**—The doctrine of materialism says that nothing exists except matter and it is movements and modifications. Even our thoughts and emotions, our mind and will are matter. This philosophical belief system devalues people and rejects the reality of the spiritual.

WHAT DOES THE BIBLE SAY?

GOD created Space, Matter and Time on the first day (Gen 1:1-5)

- space—Heaven.
- matter—Earth.
- time—The evening and the morning made the first day.

God values man because he is his crowning creative achievement. God created Adam and Eve after his image and gave them authority over all the earth. Adam became a living being when God breathed his breath into him.

- **Humanism** is a philosophy that began in medieval Europe and emphasizes the value of humans and dethrones God. Humanism supposedly prefers critical thinking and evidence over dogma and superstition. Of course to the humanist, God is the superstition. Humanism denies the existence of a creator and claims that man is god and man can achieve world peace and harmony on his own. The foundation of modern humanism is the theory of evolution.

WHAT DOES THE BIBLE SAY?

The scripture declares that God is the creator of all things; He is the Master and therefore all will give an account of his life before him (Gen 1; Rev 20). An unrepentant man does not like to retain God in his knowledge (Rom 1).

- **Pluralism** declares that there are many paths to God. Each is free to follow whatever way he may deem appropriate for himself. All philosophies are considered acceptable except Christianity because of its absolutes. It is not all inclusive. Believers in Christ are considered ignorant and bigoted. Pluralists believe that truth is subjective dependent upon each person and there are no absolute truths.

Hmmm, Can they be absolutely sure?

WHAT DOES THE BIBLE SAY?

The book of Proverbs says that men think a certain way is right because it appears to be, but at the end of it is death (Pro16:25). Jesus declared I Am the way to God (Joh 14:6). That is an absolute the philosophy of the world cannot tolerate.

- **Spiritualism** is based on the belief that the spirits of the dead still exist and can communicate with the living. The spirit world is considered a place where spirits continue to evolve.

WHAT DOES THE BIBLE SAY?

The Bible calls talking to the dead necromancy, and God forbids it. In (Deu 18:9-14) God warns his people about following after the beliefs of the nations. His word tells us we will die once and then judged by those things we have done on earth (Heb 9:27). He is still warning us today not to compromise the truth of God's word or be deceived by doctrines of demons. The spirits of the dead are confined, and there is no escape (Luk 16:19-31). Only God has the power to raise them.

- **The pseudoscience of Evolution** is the belief that all forms of life evolved from non-life in the primordial soup made from rocks and chemicals that rained down upon them. That with the magical ingredient of time, i.e., millions of years, one kind can change into another kind, i.e., a reptile changing into a bird through mutation, genetic recombination, and other sources of genetic variation.

WHAT DOES THE BIBLE SAY?

God was the creator of the Heavens and the Earth and everything that is in them. He made every living thing to bring forth after its kind (Gen 1).

Mutations never add new information to the gene pool; in fact, it is the opposite: mutations are missing information. Evolution has never been observed nor has experiments ever proven the theory correct. However, we do observe in everyday life what the Bible records in Genesis; that everything brings forth after their kind.

- FYI-Science by definition is an intellectual and practical activity encompassing the systematic study of the structure and behavior of the physical and natural world **through observation and experiment.**

(Wikipedia)

Louis Pasteur through his experiments determined that life does not come from non-life but from life through generation/reproduction. The design evidenced in all creation and the order and laws of this universe cries out for a designer with an intelligence far beyond that of man. We can observe the evidence of his handiwork everywhere we look. When a man stands before God, he will have no excuse for his lack of faith, for God has shown he exists by his creation, plus God has put it within him to know. Man denies the existence of God because of the lusts of his eyes and his flesh and the pride of life (Rom 1:18-21). Jesus said they would not come to the light because their deeds are evil (Joh 3:19-20).

> **1Jn 2:15** **Love not the world,** neither the things *that are* in the world. If any man love the world, the love of the Father is not in him.

> **1Jn 2:16** For all that *is* in the world, the lust of the flesh, and the lust of the eyes, and the pride of life, is not of the Father, but is of the world.

- ☑ Examine yourself to see how social influences have shaped your thinking.

BE TRANSFORMED

Rom 12:2 And be not conformed to this world: but **be ye transformed** by the renewing of your mind, that ye may prove what *is* that good, and acceptable, and perfect, will of God.

- transform—"metamorphose", change, transfigure.

Transformation into Christ image requires the willingness to make the necessary changes. Suffering in our flesh will occur as we bring it under the authority of Christ Spirit. Our flesh rests in the hope of the promised redemption but can be trained now to discern good and evil (Heb 5:14). Preparation for suffering in the flesh begins by arming ourselves with the mind of Christ. For with the mind of Christ and the power of the Spirit we can control the flesh, thereby allowing Christ to live his life in us in this present world. If we want the things of God, if we are after the Spirit, we will set our mind on the things of the Spirit and not the flesh.

ARM YOURSELVES WITH CHRIST MIND

For the joy set before him, Jesus endured the suffering despising the shame. He looked ahead in time and saw us glorified in him. Let us look ahead to the future hope of our calling and enter into his sufferings.

1Pe 4:1 Forasmuch then as Christ hath **suffered for us in the flesh, arm yourselves likewise with the same mind:** for he that hath suffered in the flesh hath ceased from sin;

1Pe 4:2 That he no longer should live the rest of *his* time in the flesh to the lusts of men, but to the will of God.

Rom 8:6   For to be carnally minded *is* death; but to **be spiritually minded *is* life and peace.**

Rom 8:7   Because the carnal mind *is* enmity against God: for it is not subject to the law of God, neither indeed can be.

- carnal—fleshly.

WALK IN THE SPIRIT

Walking in the Spirit is not some mystical standard that we cannot attain. With the help of the Holy Spirit, we can walk with Jesus in the unseen realm of the Spirit. When we walk according to God's word, we are walking in the Spirit. Jesus said that his words are Spirit and Life (Joh 6:63).

Gal 5:16   *This* I say then, **Walk in the Spirit**, and ye shall not fulfil the lust of the flesh.

Gal 5:17   For **the flesh lusteth against the Spirit, and the Spirit against the flesh**: and these are contrary the one to the other: so that ye cannot do the things that ye would.

Gal 5:18   But if ye be led of the Spirit, ye are not under the law.

THE FRUIT OF THE SPIRIT

Gal 5:19   Now the works of the flesh are manifest, which are *these;* Adultery, fornication, uncleanness, lasciviousness.

Gal 5:20 Idolatry, witchcraft, hatred, variance, emulations, wrath, strife, seditions, heresies.

Gal 5:21 Envyings, murders, drunkenness, revellings, and such like: of the which I tell you before, as I have also told *you* in time past, that they which do such things shall not inherit the kingdom of God.

Gal 5:22 But **the fruit of the Spirit** is love, joy, peace, longsuffering, gentleness, goodness, faith.

Gal 5:23 Meekness, temperance: against such there is no law.

Gal 5:24 And they that are Christ's have crucified the flesh with the affections and lusts.

Gal 5:25 If we live in the Spirit, let us also walk in the Spirit.

Gal 5:26 Let us not be desirous of vain glory, provoking one another, envying one another.

If we set our minds on the fleshly lusts, we will gravitate toward fulfilling those carnal desires. To allow carnal thinking to persist is allowing death to work in us. Our minds must be renewed to mirror the mind of Christ which is in us through the Spirit. If we truly desire to walk in the Spirit and bear fruit, we will attend to the word of God.

As we plant God's word in our heart, the tempter comes immediately in order to take away the word. He causes some to lose faith and tempts others to be carried away with the cares, riches, and pleasures of this world. If we love this present world the love of the Father is not in us. Love of God is a fruit of the Spirit of God that has been shed abroad in our hearts. The Christian has the Holy Spirit dwelling within who helps us to bear this fruit;

love, joy, peace, long-suffering/patience, gentleness, goodness, faith, meekness/humility, temperance/self-control. Our tree should be loaded down with all the fruit of the spirit for others to taste and see that the Lord is good. A good tree produces good fruit.

> **Luk 6:43** For a good tree bringeth not forth corrupt fruit; neither doth a corrupt tree bring forth good fruit.
>
> **Luk 6:44** For every tree is known by his own fruit. For of thorns men do not gather figs, nor of a bramble bush gather they grapes.
>
> **Luk 6:45** A good man out of the good treasure of his heart bringeth forth that which is good; and an evil man out of the evil treasure of his heart bringeth forth that which is evil: for of the abundance of the heart his mouth speaketh.

Those who have the Spirit of God are sons of God, and that is how we should see one another and treat one another. God has forgotten our past lives and sins; he cast them into the sea of forgetfulness. We are new creations, and we are now bearing good fruit. We must be patient with one another and loving and kind considering that we are in Christ body together, connected by the Spirit of Christ. We should look at one another through our new identity in Jesus, in the spirit.

> **2Co 5:15** And *that* he died for all, that they which live should not henceforth live unto themselves, but unto him which died for them, and rose again.
>
> **2Co 5:16** Wherefore **henceforth know we no man after the flesh:** yea, though we have known Christ after the flesh, yet now henceforth know we *him* no more.

2Co 5:17   Therefore **if any man *be* in Christ, *he is* a new creature:** old things are passed away; behold, all things are become new.

- We are a new creature in Christ.
- We are not of this world.

THE LIGHT OF THE WORLD

Jesus has purchased such great salvation for us, but we must work it out in our lives having great respect for his suffering, and death, and the gift of life. The fear of the Lord is the beginning of wisdom, and we are called to submit to the Holy Spirit who is working in us to change our will and to help us do God's pleasure. Then we will shine forth as lights in this world holding forth the word of life.

Php 2:12   Wherefore, my beloved, as ye have always obeyed, not as in my presence only, but now much more in my absence, **work out your own salvation with fear and trembling.**

Php 2:13   For it is **God which worketh in you both to will and to do** of *his* good pleasure.

Php 2:14   Do all things without murmurings and disputings:

Php 2:15   That ye may be blameless and harmless, the sons of God, without rebuke, in the midst of a crooked and perverse nation, among whom **ye shine as lights in the world;**

Php 2:16 Holding forth the word of life; that I may rejoice in the day of Christ, that I have not run in vain, neither laboured in vain.

- We are the light of the world.

Mat 5:14 Ye are the light of the world. A city that is set on an hill cannot be hid.

Mat 5:15 Neither do men light a candle, and put it under a bushel, but on a candlestick; and it giveth light unto all that are in the house.

Mat 5:16 Let your light so shine before men, that they may see your good works, and glorify your Father which is in heaven.

We have been born from above and are not of this world any longer. Governed by the principles of the kingdom of God, we must learn to think like a spiritual man in a spiritual kingdom. Now we are children of the light not of the darkness, and we are to shine as lights in this dark world. The world will not love us even as they did not love Jesus. Though Jesus came to rescue all men from the power of darkness the world hated him because they loved darkness rather than light (Joh 3:19). Don't be discouraged by the world and be detoured from the way. The world lies in darkness and does not know the truth. It follows the false light giver, Lucifer. If being popular in the world is important to us it will be hard to stand against the social pressure. If we are to serve God, we must be prepared to be rejected by the world.

Joh 15:18 If the world hate you, ye know that it hated me before *it hated* you.

Joh 14:19 If ye were of the world, the world would love his own: but because **ye are not of the world,** but **I**

have chosen you out of the world, therefore the world hateth you.

Col 1:12 Giving thanks unto the Father, which hath made us meet to be **partakers of the inheritance of the saints in light:**

Col 1:13 Who hath **delivered us from the power of darkness,** and hath **translated** *us* **into the kingdom of his dear Son:**

Col 1:14 In whom we have redemption through his blood, *even* the forgiveness of sins:

The scripture is like a glass which reflects the glory of Christ. As we open the word of God and behold the glory of the Lord, the Spirit changes us. Depending upon the Holy Spirit revealing Christ to us is essential if we want to see his glory. By yielding to God's working of grace, we will continue to grow from glory to glory more into his likeness up until the time we receive our inheritance at the resurrection. Our cooperation is necessary for spiritual growth for we must work out this salvation in our daily life. Be assured that God is working in us, helping us conform our will and our ways to his.

2Co 3:18 But we all, with open face **beholding as in a glass the glory** of the Lord, **are changed into the same image from glory to glory,** *even* as by the Spirit of the Lord.

LESSON 5

Experiencing God

OBJECTIVE: Develop an understanding of transformation through experience.

ISAIAH'S EXPERIENCE

Isa 6:1   In the year that king Uzziah died **I saw also the Lord** sitting upon a throne, high and lifted up, and his train filled the temple.

Isa 6:2   Above it stood the seraphims: each one had six wings; with twain he covered his face, and with twain he covered his feet, and with twain he did fly.

Isa 6:3   And one cried unto another, and said, **Holy, holy, holy,** *is* the LORD of hosts: the whole earth *is* full of his glory.

Isa 6:4   And the posts of the door moved at the voice of him that cried, and the house was filled with smoke.

Isa 6:5   Then said I, Woe *is* me! for I am undone; because I *am* a man of unclean lips, and I dwell in the midst of a people of unclean lips: for **mine eyes have seen the King, the LORD of hosts.**

Isa 6:6   Then flew one of the seraphims unto me, having a live coal in his hand, *which* he had taken with the tongs from off the altar:

Isa 6:7   And he laid *it* upon my mouth, and said, Lo, this hath touched thy lips; and **thine iniquity is taken away, and thy sin purged.**

Isa 6:8   Also I heard the voice of the Lord, saying, Whom shall I send, and who will go for us? **Then said I, Here *am* I; send me.**

The Lord revealed himself to Isaiah as a High and Holy God worthy to be worshiped. His throne was high and lifted up and the skirt of his garment filled the temple. The seraphim cry out to each other Holy, Holy, Holy inspiring each other to worship the Trinity. The whole earth is full of the glory of God and declares His greatness and so should we.

Worship of God is an integral part of our relationship with him. The Son of God is this Lord who is Highly exalted, whose holy clothing unfolds in pure majesty filling his temple. Isaiah saw the Lord in his temple, and the confrontation with God's holiness caused him to repent. Confessing his sins, he also confesses his belief in the Lord. He walked away cleansed and called, forever dramatically impacted by his experience. This same God whose righteousness filled the temple in Heaven has filled our earthly temples of clay with his presence. Shall we not inspire one another to worship our Holy God who loves us and who reveals himself to us through his Holy Son? Behold God who is Holy, Holy, Holy and who takes away our sin. He is calling still, 'Whom shall I send; who will go for us?" Isaiah responded to the call and became one of the greatest prophets in the Old Testament.

PETER'S EXPERIENCE

Luk 5:3   And he entered into one of the ships, which was Simon's, and prayed him that he would thrust out a little from the land. And he sat down, and taught the people out of the ship.

Luk 5:4   Now when he had left speaking, he said unto Simon, Launch out into the deep, and let down your nets for a draught.

Luk 5:5   And Simon answering said unto him, Master, we have toiled all the night, and have taken nothing: nevertheless at thy word I will let down the net.

Luk 5:6   And when they had this done, they inclosed a great multitude of fishes: and their net brake.

Luk 5:7   And they beckoned unto *their* partners, which were in the other ship, that they should come and help them. And they came, and filled both the ships, so that they began to sink.

Luk 5:8   When Simon Peter saw *it*, he fell down at Jesus' knees, saying, Depart from me; for I am a sinful man, O Lord.

Luk 5:9   For he was astonished, and all that were with him, at the draught of the fishes which they had taken:

Luk 5:10 And so *was* also James, and John, the sons of Zebedee, which were partners with Simon. And Jesus said unto Simon, Fear not; from henceforth thou shalt catch men.

Luk 5:11 And when they had brought their ships to land, **they forsook all, and followed him.**

Peter, like Isaiah, experienced a dramatic impact from the presence of the LORD. After Peter had toiled all night, there was no catch of fish to show for his hard work. Jesus requested permission to use the ship as a platform from which to preach. Afterward, Jesus told Peter to launch out into the deep and let down his nets. Peter was obedient though he had worked hard all night and was tired. Letting down his nets Peter caught more than they could hold, so he called for his partners to help because the catch was so great. The nets of both ships filled so full of fish they broke.

Peter's experience saw the man Christ Jesus full of the Holy Presence of God. Like Isaiah Peter could say his eyes had seen the King, the LORD of Hosts and he was forever changed. After seeing the miracle done by Jesus, Peter was stricken in heart and told the Lord to depart from him for he was a sinful man. Like Isaiah, Peter confessed his sin and responded to the call forever changed by God's presence. Once a sinner lost in sin but now a fisher of all men. God is calling for more ships and more fishers of men to help bring in the catch that awaits in depths of darkness. The nets need to be let down for the souls of men lie in the balance.

SAUL'S EXPERIENCE

Saul who was a religious zealot had much training and knowledge about the Law. At that time there was no new testament, only the writings of Moses and the Prophets. Saul was a Pharisee, taught by one of the most excellent teachers of their time, Gamaliel. Although we see Gamaliel warning the Pharisees about persecuting Christ disciples, Saul became one of the early church's staunchest enemies (Act 5:34). We first see Saul as a young man in (Act 7:58) at the scene of the stoning of Stephen. He was a part of the crowd of Pharisees standing by who heard the gospel preached that day. Saul, blinded by his hatred consented to Stephens death and held the cloaks of those who stoned him. Later, believing he was doing the work of God, Saul was headed to Damascus with papers to arrest all who named the name of Jesus and bring them bound to Jerusalem.

Act 9:3   And as he journeyed, he came near Damascus: and suddenly there shined round about him a light from heaven:

Act 9:4   And he fell to the earth, and heard a voice saying unto him, Saul, Saul, why persecutest thou me?

Act 9:5   And he said, Who art thou, Lord? And the Lord said, I am Jesus whom thou persecutest: *it is* hard for thee to kick against the pricks.

Act 9:6   And he trembling and astonished said, **Lord, what wilt thou have me to do?** And the Lord *said* unto him, Arise, and go into the city, and it shall be told thee what thou must do.

Act 9:15 But the Lord said unto him, Go thy way: **for he is a chosen vessel** unto me, to bear my name before the Gentiles, and kings, and the children of Israel:

Act 9:16   For I will shew him how great things he must suffer for my name's sake.

Act 9:17   And Ananias went his way, and entered into the house; and putting his hands on him said, Brother Saul, the Lord, *even* Jesus, that appeared unto thee in the way as thou camest, hath sent me, that thou mightest **receive thy sight, and be filled with the Holy Ghost.**

Act 9:18   And immediately there fell from his eyes as it had been scales: and he received sight forthwith, and arose, and was baptized.

Act 9:19   And when he had received meat, he was strengthened. Then was Saul certain days with the disciples which were at Damascus.

Act 9:20   And straightway **he preached Christ** in the synagogues, that he is the Son of God.

Although Saul did not receive the message that day preached by Stephen, he would meet the one Stephen declared risen on the road to Damascus. Saul's experience with Christ presence made such an indelible impression that he was transformed from murderer to saint, from Saul to Paul, preaching the very message he formerly hated and for which he persecuted others.

Paul considered it a high call to not only experience the power of Jesus resurrection but also shared in his suffering. He suffered the loss of everything; his reputation, his lifestyle, his friends and even family to win Christ.

Php 3:7   But what things were gain to me, those I counted loss for Christ.

Php 3:8   Yea doubtless, and I count all things *but* loss for the excellency of the knowledge of Christ Jesus my Lord: for whom I have suffered the loss of all things, and **do count them *but* dung, that I may win Christ.**

Php 3:9   And be found in him, not having mine own righteousness, which is of the law, but that which is through the faith of Christ, the righteousness which is of God by faith:

Php 3:10 That I may **know him, and the power of his resurrection,** and the **fellowship of his sufferings,** being made conformable unto his death;

Php 3:11 If by any means I might attain unto the resurrection of the dead.

This kind of devotion did not come from general knowledge about Jesus but a transformational experience. Jesus made himself known to Saul and Saul became Paul, the great apostle to the gentiles. The impact from Paul's conversion has influenced every nation of the world down through the corridors of time. Every believer who picks up a bible to read will see words penned by Paul under the inspiration of the Holy Spirit. Words of experience and knowledge that will make an indelible impression in our souls.

COMMON RESPONSES TO GOD'S PRESENCE

- fear—fear of God is the beginning of wisdom.
- conviction—feeling of shamefulness of sin.
- worship—humbles self.
- confession of sin—acknowledgement of truth about your sins.
- confession of faith—acknowledgement of Jesus as LORD.
- response to the call—follow Jesus.

We cannot know Christ intimately by only studying or observing his creation. We can learn about him in this manner and we should, but it is not the same as experiencing his presence and having direct communication with him. The word is meant to reveal God that we might know him, experience him and have a loving relationship with him.

FALSE OR RELIGIOUS EXPERIENCE

Some of the saddest words spoken will be to those who claimed to know Christ Jesus and to have done marvelous works in his name, but in reality, they did not. In the day of judgment, Jesus will declare that their works were wicked and that he never knew them. Jesus never knew them, so they were never saved. They may have accented to the claims that he was the Christ, but even the devils believe, and yet they tremble (Jas 2:19). Jesus said, "you must be born again (Joh 3:3)."

> Mat 7:19 Every tree that bringeth not forth good fruit is hewn down, and cast into the fire.
>
> Mat 7:20 Wherefore **by their fruits** ye shall know them.
>
> Mat 7:21 Not every one that saith unto me, Lord, Lord, shall enter into the kingdom of heaven; but **he that doeth the will of my Father** which is in heaven.
>
> Mat 7:22 Many will say to me in that day, Lord, Lord, have we not prophesied in thy name? and in thy name have cast out devils? and in thy **name done many wonderful works?**
>
> Mat 7:23 And then will I profess unto them, **I never knew you:** depart from me, ye that work iniquity.

- never—not even at any time; that is never at all.

When the seven sons of Sceva tried to cast the devil out of a man in the name of Jesus that Paul preached, the devil said that he knew Jesus and Paul, but he questioned who they were. The men beaten, were stripped of their clothing and fled the scene in defeat. Not quite the result they had intended. The spirit world only responds to the name of Jesus if used legally. Jesus gave only his disciples authority and power to use his name to do mighty works and to cast out devils. He said that nothing would harm them. The devils would not be able to do to the true disciples of Jesus what they did to the seven sons of Sceva. They are entities in the spirit realm and recognize the authority of God's Kingdom when the believer invokes Jesus name.

> Act 19:13   Then certain of the vagabond Jews, exorcists, took upon them to call over them which had evil spirits the name of the Lord Jesus, saying, We adjure you by Jesus whom Paul preacheth.
>
> Act 19:14   And there were seven sons of *one* Sceva, a Jew, *and* chief of the priests, which did so.
>
> Act 19:15   And the evil spirit answered and said, **Jesus I know, and Paul I know; but who are ye?**
>
> Act 19:16   And the man in whom the evil spirit was leaped on them, and overcame them, and prevailed against them, so that they fled out of that house naked and wounded.
>
> Act 19:17   And this was known to all the Jews and Greeks also dwelling at Ephesus; and fear fell on them all, and the name of the Lord Jesus was magnified.

We can read the Bible and books by Bible scholars and commentators and learn much information regarding Christ Jesus. We could meet his family, the church, and learn about their relationship with him, yet if we have not met Jesus personally, he is someone that someone else knows. If we do not know him, we legally have no right to his name. Jesus died so that all sinners can call on his name for salvation, but the authority and power of his name is reserved for the sons of God. Let it not be said of us what God said about Israel in (Isa 29:13). They drew near him with their mouth and honored him with their lips, but they removed their hearts far from him. Paul tells those at Corinth to examine themselves to see if they were really in the faith. Unless Jesus Christ dwells within us, we cannot dwell with him. Those who know him can testify about him.

EVIDENCE OF A TRUE EXPERIENCE

- we have fellowship with him 1 Jn 1:5-6
- we know because we love the brethren 1 Jn 3:14
- we keep his commandments and dwell in him 1 Jn 3:24
- Jesus has given us his Spirit 1 Jn 4:13
- we have the witness within ourselves 1 Jn 5:10

2Co 13:5 **Examine yourselves,** whether ye be in the faith; prove your own selves. Know ye not your own selves, **how that Jesus Christ is in you, except ye be reprobates?**

- reprobate—unapproved, that is rejected, worthless, castaway.

Is there evidence that Christ Jesus is in you?

LESSON 6
Spiritual Exercise

OBJECTIVE: To understand and demonstrate essential spiritual disciplines for transformation.

BECOMING DISCIPLES

- discipline—train oneself to do something in a controlled and habitual way.

- disciple—a learner, that is a pupil.

Joh 8:31   Then said Jesus to those Jews which believed on him, If ye **continue in my word,** *then* are ye my **disciples** indeed;

Joh 8:32   And **ye shall know the truth, and the truth shall make you free.**

Becoming a disciple of Christ means that we are going to train ourselves to study his word and allow that word to perform its work of teaching doctrine, reproof, correction and instruction in righteousness (2Ti 3:16). Only those who become true disciples in Christ word walk in sound doctrine and are transformed into Christ image and made free. In order to discipline ourselves for this undertaking of transformation, it takes setting new goals for ourselves that conform to God's will and making discipleship a priority in our lives. Only then can we know his power and his glory manifested in and through us.

> **Luk 6:40** The **disciple** is not above his master: but **every one that is perfect shall be as his master.**
>
> **Luk 6:41** And **why** beholdest thou the mote that is in thy brother's eye, but perceivest not the beam that is in thine own eye?

- perfect—to complete thoroughly.

A disciple should love others as Jesus loves them. Why Jesus ask, are we looking for faults in others instead of seeing through eyes of love? Jesus does not teach us to be a fault finder, but a problem solver. Our view of looking down on others could cause a stumbling block to our discipleship. The willingness to put Christ first and obey his commandment to love is the characteristic of a true disciple.

> **Luk 14:26** If any *man* come to me, and hate not his father, and mother, and wife, and children, and brethren, and sisters, yea, and his own life also, **he cannot be my disciple.**
>
> **Luk 14:27** And whosoever doth not bear his cross, and come after me, **cannot be my disciple.**

As disciples we are striving to be like the Master, learning from him as much as possible. Taking the message of the cross to the world is our mission, following him even to death if necessary. If we love anyone above him, we cannot be his disciple. The commandment is to love the Lord our God with all our heart, with all our strength and our brother as ourselves. Jesus demands our total loyalty and love.

> Mat 16:24 Then said Jesus unto his disciples, If any *man* will come after me, **let him deny himself, and take up his cross, and follow me.**

> Mat 16:25 For whosoever will save his life shall lose it: and whosoever will lose his life for my sake shall find it.

STUDY

> 2Ti 2:15 **Study to shew thyself approved** unto God, a workman that needeth not to be ashamed, rightly dividing the word of truth.

- study—make effort, be prompt or earnest.
- approved—properly acceptable, tried.
- workman—toiler, teacher, laborer.
- rightly dividing—(expound) correctly (the divine message).

> 2Ti 3:16 All scripture *is* given by inspiration of God, and *is* **profitable for doctrine, for reproof, for correction, for instruction in righteousness:**

2Ti 3:17 That the man of God may be perfect, throughly furnished unto all good works.

A time will come when men will not endure sound doctrine and false prophets will deceive many (2Ti 4:3-4). The disciple of Christ will learn to discern the lies and walk in truth because we have an unction, an anointing from the Holy One and know all things. All scripture is given by inspiration of the Holy Spirit and it is he who is the anointing in us (1Jn 2:18-20). In order to fulfill our call to preach the word, to speak sound doctrine, we must first learn it with the help of the Holy Spirit. With his help, we can discern spiritual things with spiritual (1Co 2:13).

1Jn 2:20 But **ye have an unction** from the Holy One, and **ye know all things**.

Tit 2:1 But speak thou the things which become **sound doctrine**:

MEDITATION

Meditation of God's word accompanies the study of his word. As we think about it and question its meaning, and embrace its truth, the Holy Spirit opens its mystery to us. Biblical meditation is a practice of thinking on the word of God and can be done anywhere at any time of day, unlike studying the bible. Meditation by cults attempt to empty the mind but that is dangerous, leaving one open to demonic possession. God gave us a mind to use and does not want us to make it blank or empty or fill it with vanities, but instead saturate it with God's word. Joshua was told by Moses to meditate the word of God day and night and he would be prosperous and have good success. After we study the word and think about it and talk about it with others we shall be able to do what is written in it. Our way shall be prosperous and we shall be successful. Like Joshua, we can be strong and courageous in our calling because we abide in his word and his word abides in us. He is with us wherever we go.

Jos 1:8 This book of the law shall not depart out of thy mouth; but thou **shalt meditate therein day and night, that thou mayest observe to do** according to all that is written therein: for **then thou shalt make thy way prosperous, and then thou shalt have good success.**

Jos 1:9 Have not I commanded thee? **Be strong and of a good courage;** be not afraid, neither be thou dismayed: for the LORD thy God *is* with thee whithersoever thou goest.

Psa 49:3 My mouth shall speak of wisdom; and the **meditation** of my heart *shall be* of **understanding.**

Psa 119:99 I have more **understanding** than all my teachers: for thy testimonies *are* my **meditation.**

Psa 1:1 Blessed *is* **the man** that walketh not in the counsel of the ungodly, nor standeth in the way of sinners, nor sitteth in the seat of the scornful.

Psa 1:2 But his delight *is* in the law of the LORD; and **in his law doth he meditate day and night.**

Meditation upon the word of God will take us to depths in the Spirit where we will drink from the deepest of God's well. Therein lies the revelation of God's glory and majesty and holiness. Therein lies the treasures of God's kingdom hidden and laid up for the children of God to discover. If we meditate (think upon) the word of God, upon things that are true, honest, just, pure, lovely, and of a good report we will stand strong. If there is any virtue or any praise we are to meditate on these things and seek wisdom and understanding that we might know more of God.

Pro 2:2   So that thou **incline thine ear unto wisdom,** *and* **apply thine heart to understanding;**

Pro 2:3   Yea, if thou criest after knowledge, *and* liftest up thy voice for understanding;

Pro 2:4   If thou **seekest** her as silver, and searchest for her as *for* hid treasures;

Pro 2:5   Then shalt thou **understand** the fear of the LORD, **and find t**he knowledge of God.

Pro 2:6   For the LORD giveth wisdom: out of his mouth *cometh* knowledge and understanding.

Php 4:6   Be careful for nothing; but in every thing by prayer and supplication with thanksgiving let your requests be made known unto God.

Php 4:7   And the peace of God, which passeth all understanding, shall keep your hearts and minds through Christ Jesus.

Php 4:8   Finally, brethren, whatsoever things are true, whatsoever things *are* honest, whatsoever things *are* just, whatsoever things *are* pure, whatsoever things *are* lovely, whatsoever things *are* of good report; if *there be* any virtue, and if *there be* any praise, **think on these things.**

Psa 104:34   **My meditation of him** shall be sweet: I will be glad in the LORD.

The mind is a powerful thing, with a will, emotions, thoughts, and imagination. Imagination is how we think ahead and also how we interpret situations. We use our ideas and creativity daily and how we use our mind determines our attitudes and our emotions.

Meditation helps to discipline the mind by not allowing it to wander into the danger zones where the devil will get an advantage and establish a place (stronghold) in us. The danger zone is where we allow our mind to be overrun and overcome with destructive imaginations and emotions. That is why we are to capture our thoughts and bring them under the obedience of Christ. Engaging the mind to meditate upon the word of God and the things that are good will cause us to have discernment, be strong in faith and will bring success.

    1Ti 4:13   Till I come, **give attendance** to reading, to exhortation, to doctrine.

    1Ti 4:14   **Neglect not the gift** that is in thee, which was given thee by prophecy, with the laying on of the hands of the presbytery.

    1Ti 4:15   **Meditate upon these things; give thyself wholly to them; that thy profiting may appear to all.**

Giving attention to hear the wisdom of God's word provides the Holy Spirit opportunity to teach us. If we neglect the study of God's word, we will not grow in knowledge and understanding. Study and meditation are ways of inclining our ears to hear and applying our heart to understand. The profiting of God's word will be evident to ourselves and others as we give ourselves entirely to the call of God on our life.

JOURNALING

Along with study and meditation, some people find it helpful to keep a journal. Keeping a journal of our studies will help us remember the word as taught to us by the Spirit. Journaling can help in expressing thoughts and feelings that some find it hard to articulate otherwise. Recording our thoughts, prayers, and dreams and keeping a record of God's answers can serve to help remember and will add fuel to the fire of our faith. The goal to become like Jesus is the primary goal of all spiritual discipline.

PRAYER

HOUSE OF PRAYER

Mat 21:13 And said unto them, It is written, **My house shall be called the house of prayer**; but ye have made it a den of thieves.

Jesus said that his father's house will be called a house of prayer. In the temple which is a type and shadow of the heavenly habitation of God, there was an altar of incense where blood was sprinkled and incense was offered up. The blood of the lamb symbolized the blood of Jesus our mediator that our prayers might be accepted. The incense ascends with the prayers of the saints that come up before God as a sweet smelling aroma. To our Father we are made a sweet smelling savor of Christ (2Co 2:15). When our Father hears our prayers in Jesus name he hears us even as his pure and holy son. As his temple we are to be a house of prayer.

Jesus sprinkled his blood on the altar and all the vessels in the holy place in Heaven and stands before God as our High Priest ever interceding for us. When we draw near by the blood of Jesus with a true heart and pray in his name we shall find favor and obtain mercy (Heb 4:16).

1Co 3:16 Know ye not that **ye are the temple of God**, and *that* the Spirit of God dwelleth in you?

ASK IN JESUS NAME

Joh 15:13   And whatsoever ye shall **ask in my name,** that will I do, that the Father may be glorified in the Son.

Joh 15:14 If ye shall ask any thing **in my name, I will do** *it.*

Joh 15:15   Ye have not chosen me, but I have chosen you, and ordained you, that ye should go and bring forth fruit, and *that* your fruit should remain: that whatsoever ye shall **ask of the Father in my name**, he may give it you.

Joh 16:23   And in that day ye shall ask me nothing. Verily, verily, I say unto you, **Whatsoever ye shall ask the Father in my name, he will give** *it* **you.**

Joh 16:24   **Hitherto have ye asked nothing in my name**: ask, and ye shall receive, that your joy may be full.

When Jesus was with the disciples he prayed to the Father for them but now at the nearness of his time to be offered up, He was preparing them for his departure. They must learn to trust the Father for themselves and discover the power of praying in the name of Jesus. Jesus made way for us all to go directly to the Father through his flesh and blood. His body bore our sins unto death, and then his body raised without sin. He entered into the temple of God in heaven, and as our High Priest, he sprinkled his blood on the mercy seat (Heb 9:12, 23-24). He then sat down on the right hand of God the Father. Now we can come boldly to the throne of grace in Heaven in Jesus name and find joy in knowing and receiving favor from our Heavenly Father. Since Jesus, our brother understands our infirmities he knows how to help. God's amazing grace provides this privilege of being chosen and invited to come boldly to the throne room. We may come and drink freely of the fountain of the water of life at his throne (Rev 21:6).

Heb 4:14 Seeing then that we have **a great high priest**, that is passed into the heavens, Jesus the Son of God, let us hold fast *our* profession.

Heb 4:15 For we have not an high priest which cannot be **touched with the feeling of our infirmities;** but was in all points tempted like as *we are, yet* without sin.

Heb 4:16 Let us therefore **come boldly unto the throne of grace,** that we may obtain mercy, and find grace to help in time of need.

ASK ACCORDING TO THE WORD / GOD'S WILL

God desires to give us the blessings of his kingdom, and He has chosen us and ordained that we bear fruit. According to the parable of the sower in (Mat 13), first, the word must be planted in our hearts in good ground and allowed to grow. The seed (the Word of truth) needs to be watered by the rain (God's Spirit). Jesus said the time has come that true worshippers worship in spirit and truth. If we abide in him and his truth abides in us, then we can ask what we will, and God will do it. His word reveals his will, and when we pray for his will, submitting our own to him, he honors our prayer. We can be confident that if we ask anything according to the will of God, he will hear our prayers and give us what we ask.

Joh 15:7 **If ye abide in me, and my words abide in you,** ye shall **ask** what ye will, and it shall be done unto you.

1Jn 5:13 These things have I written unto you that believe on the name of the Son of God; that ye may know that ye have eternal life, and that ye may believe on the name of the Son of God.

1Jn 5:14 And this is **the confidence** that we have **in him**, that, **if we ask any thing according to his will, he heareth us:**

1Jn 5:15 And if we know that he hear us, whatsoever we ask, we know that we have the petitions that we desired of him.

Joh 4:23 But the hour cometh, and now is, when the true worshippers shall **worship the Father in spirit and in truth:** for the Father seeketh such to worship him.

Joh 4:24 God *is* a Spirit: and they that worship him **must worship** *him* **in spirit and in truth.**

HOW TO PRAY

When He was on earth, Jesus would seek out solitary places where he could pray. The disciples took note that he prayed often and they ask him how to pray. He told his disciples first of all not to be hypocritical; wanting just to be seen and to have the honor of men. There is an honor that comes from seeking a relationship with our Father in a quiet or secret place.

Mat 6:5 And when thou prayest, thou shalt not be as the hypocrites *are:* for they love to pray standing in the synagogues and in the corners of the streets, that they may be seen of men. Verily I say unto you, They have their reward.

Mat 6:6 But thou, **when thou prayest, enter into thy closet,** and when thou hast shut thy door, pray **to thy Father which is in secret;** and thy Father which seeth in secret shall reward thee openly.

Prayer is honest communication with our Holy Heavenly Father who has all knowledge and power. In that secret place of the Most High, we find refuge under the shadow of his wings (Psa 91).

Psa 91:1 He that dwelleth in **the secret place of the most High** shall abide under the shadow of the Almighty.

Psa 91:2 I will say of the LORD, *He is* my **refuge and my fortress**: my God; in him will I trust.

In the Secret place, we have communion with the living God in Spirit and truth. It is the place to seek the Father's blessing over our lives, and the place of his love poured out in manifest glory in Christ. A place where we can worship, confess our sins, and pour out our hearts to him in earnest supplication. Dwelling in the secret place with God there is no fear; only love, peace and rest for our souls. We are never alone when we are in solitude with our God but without God solitude is lonely. Speaking of Israel, God said that in returning to him they will find rest and salvation; and in quietness and confidence in God, they will find strength (Isa 30:15). Returning to the God of our salvation and resting in his love and being still and knowing in confidence that he is God will add to our strength. Knowing him in oneness in fellowship and dwelling in his presence absorbing his Spirit and Life is as necessary as breathing to walk in his power. We are joined to the Lord and are one spirit. The Life of God will permeate everything we do if we allow God to be God in us. Being still and allowing God to speak and manifest himself will bring life to our words as they become fitly spoken under the Master's control. Seeking the Lord in the stillness of the secret place will help us learn to control the tongue as we not only pour out our heart but listen for his voice. God desires our intellectual, emotional and spiritual communication but he will not hear for our much speaking. He knows our heart and what we need, so there is no need for useless repetitions. Our Father's takes good pleasure in giving us the kingdom. He offers what is his to us because He is good.

> **Mat 6:7** But when ye pray, use not vain repetitions, as the heathen *do:* for they think that they shall be heard for their much speaking.

> **Mat 6:8** Be not ye therefore like unto them: for **your Father knoweth** what things ye have need of, before ye ask him.

We will find there is freedom in submitting to his will in total reliance on him. Whom the Son sets free is free indeed. The new spirit man's desire within is freedom to reign in life. We can trust God as our daily sustenance, both physical and spiritual. The wisdom, the riches, the power and the authority of Christ kingdom is brought to bear on our circumstances on earth as we pray in faith with thanksgiving glorifying his name. His righteousness is ours, and in him, we shall reign if we keep his commandments. The Father wills to give us the kingdom (Luk 12:32).

God's love forgives when it is not deserved, and we are to love as he loves. Unforgiveness is a stumbling block to ourselves and others, and it gives place for the devil to get an advantage over us. God leads us away from temptation, but Satan lures and entices into temptation. Attraction of all vices will come through the devil, the tempter of the brethren, as he begins to kill, steal, and destroy. However, no temptation has come upon us that is not common to man, but with all temptation, God makes a way to escape (1Co 10:13). The pathway of escape from the snare of un-forgiveness is the decision to walk in God's light and obey his command to love (1Jn 1:7). Then we can be forgiven and cleansed of the bitterness of unforgiveness in the blood of Christ and have fellowship with one another.

Mat 6:9   After this manner therefore pray ye: Our Father which art in heaven, Hallowed be thy name.

Mat 6:10   Thy kingdom come. Thy will be done in earth, as *it is* in heaven.

Mat 6:11   Give us this day our daily bread.

Mat 6:12   And forgive us our debts, as we forgive our debtors.

Mat 6:13   And lead us not into temptation, but deliver us from evil: **For thine is the kingdom, and the power, and the glory, for ever. Amen.**

Mat 6:14   For if ye forgive men their trespasses, your heavenly Father will also forgive you:

Mat 6:15   But if ye forgive not men their trespasses, neither will your Father forgive your trespasses.

1Jn 1:7   But if we walk in the light, as he is in the light, we have fellowship one with another, and the blood of Jesus Christ his Son cleanseth us from all sin.

FASTING

The fast is meant to bring our heart, mind, and body under control of God so that we might be loosed from bands of wickedness, from heavy burdens and oppression and every yoke of bondage. Fasting is also to help us show mercy, to stop pointing the accusing finger and speaking vain words. Then our light will break out and our health will spring forth quickly, and our righteousness in Christ will lead us and God will protect us. If we love others and act in mercy instead of judgment and use our tongue for blessing instead of speaking vain things God will answer when we call. Fasting will help to loosen us from every weight and sin that we might help to free others. Freely we have received and freely we shall give.

Isa 58:6 *Is* not this **the fast that I have chosen?** to loose the bands of wickedness, to undo the heavy burdens, and to let the oppressed go free, and that ye break every yoke?

Isa 58:7 *Is it* not to deal thy bread to the hungry, and that thou bring the poor that are cast out to thy house? when thou seest the naked, that thou cover him; and that thou hide not thyself from thine own flesh?

Isa 58:8 Then shall thy light break forth as the morning, and **thine health shall spring forth** speedily: and **thy righteousness shall go before thee; the glory of the LORD shall be thy rereward.**

Isa 58:9 Then shalt thou call, and the LORD shall answer; thou shalt cry, and he shall say, Here I *am*. **If thou take away from the midst of thee the yoke, the putting forth of the finger, and speaking vanity;**

Those who make pretense and fast and pray before men to appear holy already have received the reward of the honor of men. If we want the recognition that comes from God, we will follow Jesus instructions and fast in secret before our God. God who sees secretly will honor us openly.

There were times of corporate fast such as when Israel fasted on days of Holy Convocation appointed by God, and when the disciples fasted while waiting for the promise of the Spirit at Pentecost. The washing of the face and anointing the head consecrates you for the fast before God.

Mat 6:16 Moreover **when ye fast**, be not, as the hypocrites, of a sad countenance: for they disfigure their faces, that they may appear unto men to fast. Verily I say unto you, They have their reward.

Mat 6:17 But thou, **when thou fastest, anoint thine head, and wash thy face;**

Mat 6:18 That thou appear not unto men to fast, but unto thy Father which is in secret: and **thy Father, which seeth in secret, shall reward thee openly.**

Jesus fasted forty days and nights in the wilderness being tempted by the devil. He defeated Satan and returned in power and began to preach, heal, cast out devils and do all manner of miracles (Luk 4). When Jesus, Peter, James, and John came down from the Mount where Jesus transfigured, they found the disciples arguing with the religious leaders. The disciples were unable to cast a devil out of a boy, and his father was distraught and turned to Jesus and begged for help. Jesus cast out the devil, and later the disciples ask him why they could not cast it out. Jesus said it was because of unbelief; however, this kind does not come out but by prayer and fasting. Fasting serves to get carnality and disbelief out of us and then we can get the strongest of spirits out of others.

Luk 4:1 And Jesus being full of the Holy Ghost returned from Jordan, and was **led by the Spirit** into the wilderness.

Luk 4:2 Being forty days tempted of the devil. And in those days **he did eat nothing:** and when they were ended, he afterward hungered.

When Jesus ended the fast, his first encounter was with the devil. He met the full weight of Satan's power coming at him in all manner of temptation. He wielded the word of God like a sword and defeated his enemy. Afterward, he was ministered to by angels. When Jesus came out of the wilderness, he came out full of the Holy Ghost and power. Any time we endeavor to draw closer to God, the devil tries to thwart the work of the Spirit within us. We too can expect to be met with opposition: spirits of oppression. Afterward, we shall be ministered to also by angels and walk in the power of the Spirit.

TO GET RID OF UNBELIEF

Mat 17:19   Then came the disciples to Jesus apart, and said, Why could not we cast him out?

Mat 17:20   And Jesus said unto them, **Because of your unbelief:** for verily I say unto you, If ye have **faith as** a grain of mustard seed, ye shall say unto this mountain, Remove hence to yonder place; and it shall remove; and nothing shall be impossible unto you.

Mat 17:21   **Howbeit this kind goeth not out but by prayer and fasting.**

TO ORDAIN INTO THE MINISTRY

The early church ministered to the Lord in worship, and praise and they prayed and fasted. The disciples were fasting and praying when they selected Matthias to take Judas' place by drawing lots (Act 1:16-26). Also in (Act 13) the disciples were worshipping and fasting and praying when Holy Spirit spoke and said that Barnabas and Saul were to be separated; consecrated, anointed for the work of Apostles.

The instruction to lay hands on Barnabas and Saul to be added to the number of Apostles may have been a bit surprising to them. Many teach that there were no apostles after the twelve apostles except Matthias. Although men may protest because it does not line up with their theology, it is clear Barnabas and Saul were Apostles (Act 14:14). At this point there are 14 apostles and more will be added to take the gospel to the ends of the earth. Paul and Barnabas were apostles to the Gentiles.

> Act 13:2   As **they ministered to the Lord, and fasted,** the Holy Ghost said, **Separate me Barnabas and Saul for the work** whereunto I have called them.

> Act 13:3   And **when they had fasted and prayed, and laid** *their* **hands on them,** they sent *them* away.

> Act 14:23   And when they had **ordained them elders** in every church, and had **prayed with fasting,** they commended them to the Lord, on whom they believed.

TO BRING THE BODY UNDER SUBJECTION

Not only did the body of Christ fast and pray corporately but individually as well. Perhaps that is one of the reasons they turned the world upside down. Concerning husband and wife, when fasting from intimate relations, it should be with the consent of the spouse. It is not commanded to fast.

> 1Co 9:26   I therefore so run, not as uncertainly; so fight I, not as one that beateth the air:

> 1Co 9:27   But **I keep under my body, and bring** *it* **into subjection:** lest that by any means, when I have preached to others, I myself should be a castaway.

> 1Co 7:4   The wife hath not power of her own body, but the husband: and likewise also the husband hath not power of his own body, but the wife.

1Co 7:5   Defraud ye not one the other, **except *it be* with consent for a time, that ye may give yourselves to fasting and prayer;** and come together again, that Satan tempt you not for your incontinency.

1Co 7:6   But I speak this by permission, *and* **not of commandment.**

You are so very important to the work of God no matter the work you are called to do. Because of Pauls call it was vital that he kept watch and often fast because of such grave circumstances he faced. He said he must keep his body under subjection to the spirit so that he can fight the good fight of faith with certainty to win, not just take swings (try) at it. Prayer and fasting are a means of doing that. Are we approved as the minister of God in patience, in afflictions, in needs, in distresses, in persecutions, troubles, labor, watching (staying awake, alert in prayer) and fasting? Most have not faced such perils as Paul, yet we must be prepared if and when they come.

2Co 6:4   But in all *things* **approving ourselves as the ministers** of God, in much patience, in afflictions, in necessities, in distresses.

2Co 6:5   In stripes, in imprisonments, in tumults, in labours, **in watchings, in fastings;**

GOALS

- goal—An idea of the future or desired result that a person envisions and plans and commits to achieve

Php 3:10   **That I may know him,** and the power of his resurrection, and the fellowship of his sufferings, being made conformable unto his death;

Php 3:11 If by any means I might attain unto the resurrection of the dead.

Php 3:12 Not as though I had already attained, either were already perfect: but **I follow after, if that I may apprehend** that for which also I am apprehended of Christ Jesus.

Php 3:13 Brethren, I count not myself to have apprehended: but *this* one thing *I do,* **forgetting those things which are behind, and reaching forth** unto those things which are before.

Php 3:14 **I press toward the mark for the prize** of the **high calling of God in** Christ Jesus.

Php 3:15 Let us therefore, **as many as be perfect, be thus minded:** and if in any thing ye be otherwise minded, God shall reveal even this unto you.

- conformable—to render like, to assimilate.
- apprehend—take eagerly, seize, possess.
- press—to pursue.
- mark—goal.
- high—upward.
- calling—invitation.

Pauls goal was to know Christ, the power of his resurrection and the fellowship of his suffering and to be faithful like Christ unto his death. Everyone who follows Christ should have these same goals. So many set their sight on human achievements to receive honor from men. The purpose of the upward call is to have a more in-depth knowledge of Christ and receive the praise that can only come from God: to hear God say, "Well done, good and faithful servant." For that to happen, we must stop looking at the things behind us, set our focus on the prize and reach for the destiny God has set before us; the good work we were created to do in Christ Jesus.

As we press toward the mark set before us, we see Jesus encouraging us to continue in the faith in pursuit of the joy that lies ahead. He is our example to follow, and as we have a relationship with him, in submission to him, he lives his life through us. With Jesus in control, we shall obtain the prize of our high calling.

Is your heart and mind set on these goals for your life?

PREPARE YOUR HEART TO SEEK

Heb 12:1   Wherefore seeing we also are compassed about with so great a cloud of witnesses, let us **lay aside every weight, and the sin** which doth so easily beset *us*, and let us **run with patience the race that is set before us.**

Heb 12:2   **Looking unto Jesus** the author and finisher of *our* faith; who **for the joy that was set before him endured the cross**, despising the shame, and is set down at the right hand of the throne of God.

Heb 12:3   For **consider him** that endured such contradiction of sinners against himself, lest ye be wearied and faint in your minds.

Jesus, for the joy set before him, endured the suffering of the cross despising the shame. He fixed his eyes on the goal as did his Father. God looked ahead to see Christ seed (his generation); those that would be born again as a result of Christ atonement.

Isa 53:10 Yet it pleased the LORD to bruise him; he hath put *him* to grief: when thou shalt make **his soul an offering for sin, he shall see** *his* **seed,** he shall prolong *his* days, and the pleasure of the LORD shall prosper in his hand.

Christ kept his eyes on the prize of the high calling in his life. He was out to accomplish something, to be master over sin and death in man's stead thus destroying the works of the devil. We are to consider his victory over sin and death and then exercise that dominion in our life. We can run this race with patience when we consider that Jesus has gone before us, and there is a fullness of joy that awaits.

Let's look to Christ Jesus as our inspiration and strength knowing it is he, the author and the finisher of our faith who dwells in us: living his life in us (Gal 2:20). Looking ahead to the future gives us a hope that causes us to exercise faith in God and to live for him. He will reward us if we seek him diligently.

Heb 11:6 But without faith *it is* impossible to please *him:* for he that cometh to God **must believe that he is, and** *that* **he is a rewarder of them that diligently seek him.**

King Rehoboam was reigning in his own wisdom and the Lord said he did evil in not preparing his heart to seek the Lord. He did not consider the reward of knowing God nor the honor that comes from him.

2Ch 12:14 And he did evil, because he **prepared not his heart** to seek the LORD.

David advised his son Solomon to set his heart and soul to seek God: to make the decision about serving him with his whole heart and depend on his wisdom and power. Solomon, the son of David, was a man of peace, and he would be the one to build the temple of the Lord in Jerusalem. His father was giving him wise advice that we too would do well to heed. David was a man of prayer who himself was after God's own heart. We have a record of his prayers and songs of worship that reveal God to us. As a musician, David's anointed playing had the power to cast out evil spirits, and when the Philistines defied Saul's army, David was the only one with the courage to fight Goliath. David made the decision early in life to seek and serve God. His position in life and all he possessed was given him by God who rewards those who diligently seek him.

1Ch 22:19 Now set your heart and your soul to seek the LORD your God; **arise** therefore, and **build ye the sanctuary of the LORD God,** to bring the ark of the covenant of the LORD, and the holy vessels of God, into the house that is to be built to the name of the LORD.

1Pe 2:25 Ye also, as **lively stones, are built up** a **spiritual house,** an holy priesthood, to offer up spiritual sacrifices, acceptable to God by Jesus Christ.

Let us set our hearts and souls to seek the Lord our God diligently, and then let us rise and build the sanctuary of the Lord with living stones. We bring Jesus and the Holy Spirit of God to others through the preaching of the gospel that others may become part of God's sanctuary. As a holy priesthood, we offer up spiritual sacrifices to God of worship and praise because He is worthy of all honor. As we humble ourselves before God and seek to know him, he rewards us and reveals himself to us. He wants us to know that the Lord Jesus is God and that he will be exalted.

1Pe 2:9 But ye *are* a chosen generation, **a royal priesthood,** an holy nation, a peculiar people; that ye should **shew forth the praises** of him who hath called you out of darkness into his marvelous light:

Psa 46:10 **Be still, and know that I *am* God: I will be exalted** among the heathen, I will be exalted in the earth.

Psa 100:1 A Psalm of praise. Make a joyful noise unto the LORD, all ye lands.

Psa 100:2 Serve the LORD with gladness: **come before his presence** with singing.

Psa 100:3 **Know ye that the LORD he *is* God:** *it is* he *that* hath made us, and not we ourselves; *we are* his people, and the sheep of his pasture.

Psa 100:4 Enter into his gates with thanksgiving, *and* into his courts with praise: **be thankful unto him, *and* bless his name.**

In Psalm 100 we are told to make a joyful noise to the Lord with singing, knowing He is God, but in (Psa 46) we are told to be still and know that he is God. In the first instance, we can know God our creator by humbling ourselves and giving him thanks, praise and honor as we approach his throne joyfully. In the second instance, we can find him in the surrender of stillness listening for his voice, feeling the weight of his glory as we sit in his presence. In both cases, the beauty of the Lord manifests that we might know him. In (Joh 14:21) Jesus said that he would manifest himself to those who love him. It is our love for him that stirs our desire to behold him and his glory.

As we seek to behold his splendor and to know him, we put ourselves in a position to receive from his goodness. Instead of just hearing about him, we can fellowship with him, and his life will be manifested to us and in us.

Psa 27:4 One *thing* have I desired of the LORD, **that will I seek after;** that I may dwell in the house of

> the LORD all the days of my life, to behold the **beauty** of the LORD, and to enquire in his temple.

> **1Jn 1:2** (For the life was manifested, and we have seen *it*, and bear witness, and shew unto you that eternal life, which was with the Father, and was manifested unto us;)

> **1Jn 1:3** That which we have seen and heard declare we unto you, that **ye also may have fellowship with us:** and truly our fellowship *is* with the Father, and with his Son Jesus Christ.

In (Eph 2:22) it says that we being built together a spiritual house for a habitation of God. We are meant to fellowship with the Father and the Son in the temple of God. There are souls that need to hear the gospel, and we are called into the harvest to work. We must be willing, determined, and prepared for the work we have been ordained to do. It starts at the Master's feet seeking his fellowship and his wisdom through prayer, thanksgiving, praise, and learning his word. As we ask God, he will open up to us the mysteries of the kingdom of God (Matt 13). God created us to be intellectual, emotional, creative and inquisitive beings and He delights in engaging us emotionally and intellectually. He will give us answers if we ask. The Holy Spirit can open our mind to receive great knowledge if we will delight in knowing God. He enjoys sharing his kingdom with us and its mysteries.

> **Luk 11:9** And I say unto you, **Ask**, and it shall be given you; **seek**, and ye shall find; **knock**, and it shall be opened unto you.

> **Luk 11:10** For every one that asketh receiveth; and he that seeketh findeth; and to him that knocketh it shall be opened.

MARTHA AND MARY

Martha invited Jesus to her home where she lived with her sister Mary. Mary sat down at Jesus' feet to hear his teaching with his disciples but Martha her sister was very busy serving her guests and became offended that her sister was not helping.

> Luk 10:38   Now it came to pass, as they went, that he entered into a certain village: and a certain woman named Martha received him into her house.
>
> Luk 10:39   And she had a sister called **Mary, which also sat at Jesus' feet, and heard his word.**
>
> Luk 10:40   But **Martha was cumbered about much serving,** and came to him, and said, **Lord, dost thou not care** that my sister hath left me to serve alone? bid her therefore that she help me.
>
> Luk 10:41   And Jesus answered and said unto her, Martha, Martha, thou art careful and troubled about many things:
>
> Luk 10:42   But **one thing is needful**: and Mary hath chosen that good part, which shall not be taken away from her.

Martha confronted Jesus about his part in the offense because to her he didn't seem to care that she was left to serve alone and she wanted Jesus to tell her sister to help her. Jesus is not offended by the comment but reveals that Martha was a worrier and troubled about many things. There were some underlying issues which led up to this moment. Martha thought that she was justified in saying what she said to Jesus. It doesn't state that she asked her sister to help before she spoke to Jesus about it, and so it is interesting to know why she wants Jesus to tell her. She was upset with Mary for not helping, and she wanted Jesus to see and acknowledge Mary's wrongdoing and correct her. Her work oriented righteousness caused her to misjudge her sister and accuse the Lord of not caring about her. Both sisters had the heart to please God, but Jesus said that Mary had chosen the best part and he would not take it from her. Jesus wants all to hear his words and receive wisdom before attempting to please him in what we believe is doing our part (Joh 6:63). We will miss the very essence of our responsibility by missing our time fellowshipping with and learning from Jesus.

Martha had it backward; she was working hard to serve others but ignorant of her own needs. She was cumbered about with much serving which means to drag all around and to distract. In this case, Martha was distracted from listening to the Master and probably was distracting others as well. Without abiding first in God's presence, it is easy to feel overwhelmed by the responsibility of serving others and begin to feel resentment. Jesus came to be the servant and Martha was missing her opportunity to receive what she needed most; words of life that would bring much-needed joy and peace. We could alleviate much stress in our own life by following Mary's example and sit at Jesus' feet allowing him to minister to us instead of worrying and fretting in every situation. After we are refreshed and built up, we can restore and build up others and accomplish the good works we have been ordained to do in his service.

Martha's mind was concentrating on fleshly things as she sought to serve and she became tired and resentful. Mary's mind was on spiritual things; she was seeking the bread of life. Jesus revealed that Martha needed rest from her many worries, even about serving him. We are invited to take Jesus yoke upon us and learn of him, and we will find the much-needed rest for our souls.

Understanding our dependence upon Christ and our responsibility to respond to his will is the key to balance in our life. Let us not get distracted by what we believe is our service for him and forget that Jesus is the source of all ministry. Jesus said that only one thing is needful and that was him.

☑ Are you spending time at Jesus feet?

RUN TO OBTAIN

1Co 9:24   Know ye not that they which run in a race run all, but one receiveth the prize? **So run, that ye may obtain.**

1Co 9:25   **And every man that striveth for the mastery is temperate in all things.** Now they *do it* to obtain a corruptible crown; but we an incorruptible.

1Co 9:26   **I therefore so run, not as uncertainly**; so fight I, not as one that beateth the air:

1Co 9:27   But I **keep under my body, and bring** *it* **into subjection**: lest that by any means, when I have preached to others, I myself should be a castaway.

Instead of being spectators, we are to enter the race and run to win Christ, striving for mastery. The struggle not only includes contending with the enemy of our soul but with our flesh as we endeavor to win the prize according to God's will. An athlete pushes his body to its fullest potential by giving his body the proper nutrition and bringing it into submission through discipline. As we learned in an earlier lesson, the flesh lusts against the spirit and the spirit against the flesh. Whichever one we feed will be the one that wins the battle. To gain mastery, we must feed the new spirit man who is in the image of Christ. Learning to be temperate is to exercise self-restraint in everything.

2Ti 2:5   And if a man also **strive for masteries,** *yet* is he not crowned, except he **strive lawfully.**

To reach the Olympics, an athlete must train his mind and his body. He must exercise faith that he can accomplish the goals he has set for himself. Then he applies the necessary self-discipline. He does this to win a crown that will perish, but we for a crown which does not perish. If an athlete breaks the rules of the game, he is disqualified and rejected. We also must win the race lawfully to obtain the crown. We can be confident in the one who called us knowing for a certainty that he is God and shall perform his word concerning us. Let us keep our eyes on the hope of glory (the prize) with confidence of what lies ahead for us and fight the good fight of faith. Remember, we live by the teaching and faith of the Son of God who loves us and he is with us walking out his life in us.

EXERCISE YOURSELF TO GODLINESS

1Ti 4:7 But refuse profane and old wives' fables, and **exercise thyself** *rather* **unto godliness.**

1Ti 4:8 For bodily exercise profiteth little: but **godliness is profitable** unto all things, having promise of the life that now is, and of that which is to come.

1Ti 4:9 This *is* **a faithful saying and worthy of all acceptation.**

1Ti 4:10 For therefore we both labour and suffer reproach, because we trust in the living God, who is the Saviour of all men, specially of those that believe.

A godly life has great profit, not just in the future but in the present. If we desire to be a true disciple (learner), we shall learn to exercise our spiritual muscles. The athlete puts himself through rigorous training bringing his body under self-restraint. In his flesh, he aches and pains yet he continues the discipline knowing that when his muscles are built and trained the flesh will find its ultimate freedom and joy in reaching its fullest potential.

God's grace teaches us to deny ungodliness and live righteously in this life and not just wait for the future. Now faith is, and the just shall live by faith. It takes daily exercise in godliness to develop the spiritual muscles of a seasoned, mature Christian whose physical senses can even discern good from evil. If we continue in the teachings of his word we are his disciples and being subject to his word, we are made free. Only by doing so can we find our ultimate freedom, reach our fullest potential, finish the race in this present world, and win the prize before us.

Heb 5:14 But strong meat belongeth to them that are of full age, *even* those who **by reason of use have their senses exercised to discern both good and evil.**

Tit 2:11 For **the grace of God** that bringeth salvation hath appeared to all men.

Tit 2:12 Teaching us that, denying ungodliness and worldly lusts, we should live soberly, righteously, and godly, in this present world;

Tit 2:13 Looking for that blessed hope, and the glorious appearing of the great God and our Saviour Jesus Christ;

Tit 2:14 Who gave himself for us, that he might **redeem** us from all iniquity, and **purify** unto himself a peculiar people, **zealous of good works.**

2Co 6:16 And what agreement hath the temple of God with idols? for **ye are the temple of the living God**; as God hath said, I will dwell in them, and walk in *them;* and I will be their God, and they shall be my people.

2Co 6:17 Wherefore **come out from among them, and be ye separate,** saith the Lord, and touch not the unclean *thing;* and I will receive you.

2Co 6:18 And will be a Father unto you, and ye shall be my sons and daughters, saith the Lord Almighty.

While we are learning spiritual disciplines, it is necessary to remind ourselves that they are meant to cultivate our relationship with our Father; not a set of legalistic rules which will only serve to bind. Jesus is made to us wisdom; he has given us his mind that we might be able to deny ungodliness and live soberly in this world. Soberly means to be of a sound mind. Our sanctification/holiness has been given to us as a gift even as Christ Righteousness has. Jesus said the truth would make men free; not the accumulation of facts, but knowledge of the truth that transforms that we might be able to live righteously and godly in this present world. He redeemed us to purify us, making us a peculiar people who would be zealous of living righteously. Since we are the temple of God where God dwells we should separate ourselves from the spirit of the world and seek that which is holy (sacred), that which has the promise of life.

- Godliness is profitable in all things and has promise of life in this present life.

LESSON 7

Holiness

OBJECTIVE: To understand and demonstrate transformation in holiness.

GOD'S HOLINESS

INCOMPARABLE

Exo 15:11   Who *is* like unto thee, O LORD, among the gods? who *is* like thee, glorious in holiness, fearful *in* praises, doing wonders?

1Sa 2:1   And Hannah prayed, and said, My heart rejoiceth in the LORD, mine horn is exalted in the LORD: my mouth is enlarged over mine enemies; because I rejoice in thy salvation.

1Sa 2:2 *There is* **none holy as the LORD: for** *there is* **none beside thee:** neither *is there* any rock like our God.

- holy—sacred.

Holiness is a divine quality expressing what is characteristic of God only and equates to his deity. In (Amos 4:2) it says that God has sworn by his holiness and in (Amos 6:8) it says the Lord has sworn by himself. Both scriptures are expressing the same meaning. To swear by his holiness, God is swearing by himself: his holiness is incomparable. He is the Holy One.

Amo 4:2 The **Lord GOD hath sworn by his holiness,** that, lo, the days shall come upon you, that he will take you away with hooks, and your posterity with fishhooks.

Isa 40:25 To whom then will ye liken me, or shall I be equal? **saith the Holy One.**

Hos 11:9 ... for I *am* God, and not man; **the Holy One in the midst of thee...**

The term "The Holy One" is one of the most frequently used titles of God by the Rabbis. There is none holy as the Lord; none can compare to him. As God, he is different from and high above his creation and though he far transcends man he is not distant from him. As God, he is pure and holy and cannot abide with sin. He is of purer eyes than to behold evil (Hab 1:13). Although God does not will that any should perish, his holiness and justice demand judgment for the wages of sin is death. When evil comes to a full measure, God brings judgment.

In the days of Noah, wickedness pervaded over the whole earth utterly corrupting man and even beast. Because the imagination of man's heart was continually evil, God brought judgment by a great flood. However, Noah found grace in the sight of God for he was a righteous man and his family was spared God's wrath upon the earth. In obedience to God's warning of judgment, Noah built an Ark whereby he and his family and many creatures escaped (Gen 6:1-6). God would start over with the generation of Noah and his sons and their wives (Gen 9).

GOD'S HOLINESS REVEALED

God's holiness manifests in his character, his name, his words, his works, and his kingdom. We are not to take his name in vain but give glory to his holy name. His holy name reflects his divine nature. God is holy. Where he sits is holy, sanctified by his holiness (Isa 6:1-3). Christ Jesus enthrones himself upon our hearts, and we are sanctified by his holiness. We are his temple.

> **Psa 22:3** But **thou *art* holy,** *O thou* that inhabitest the praises of Israel.

> **Psa 99:9** Exalt the LORD our God, and worship at his holy hill; for the LORD **our God *is* holy.**

> **Isa 57:15** For thus saith the high and lofty One that inhabiteth eternity, **whose name *is* Holy**; I dwell in the high and holy *place,* with him also *that is* of a contrite and humble spirit, to revive the spirit of the humble, and to revive the heart of the contrite ones.

> **1Ch 16:10 Glory ye in his holy name:** let the heart of them rejoice that seek the LORD.

> **Psa 60:6** God hath **spoken in his holiness;** I will rejoice, I will divide Shechem, and mete out the valley of Succoth.

Jer 23:9 Mine heart within me is broken because of the prophets; all my bones shake; I am like a drunken man, and like a man whom wine hath overcome, because of the LORD, and because of the **words of his holiness.**

Psa 145:17 The LORD *is* righteous in all his ways, and **holy in all his works.**

Psa 47:8 God reigneth over the heathen: God sitteth upon the **throne of his holiness.**

Christs' character attributes are reflected through believers as we change into his likeness, from glory to glory and strength to strength. His holiness dwells within us through the Holy One.

OUR SANCTIFICATION

1Co 1:30 But of him are ye in Christ Jesus, who of God is made unto us wisdom, and righteousness, and **sanctification,** and redemption:

- sanctification—purification, holiness.

God is calling us to be holy because he is holy. It is only possible by abiding in Christ for He is our sanctification, our holiness. Our lifestyles should be a reflection of the holiness that is in Christ. Through the new birth, the believer becomes a holy temple of God, and as we put on the new man, we are putting on the righteousness and true holiness of God. Jesus said we are clean through the word, sanctified by the truth.

1Co 3:16 Know ye not that ye are the temple of God, and *that* the Spirit of God dwelleth in you?

1Co 3:17 If any man defile the temple of God, him shall God destroy; for **the temple of God is holy, which** *temple* **ye are.**

1Pe 1:13 Wherefore gird up the loins of your mind, be sober, and hope to the end for the grace that is to be brought unto you at the revelation of Jesus Christ;

1Pe 1:14 As obedient children, not fashioning yourselves according to the former lusts in your ignorance:

1Pe 1:15 But as he which hath called you is holy, so **be ye holy in all manner of conversation;**

1Pe 1:16 Because it is written, **Be ye holy; for I am holy.**

Although we are called to separate from the ungodly ways of the world, we are not called to separate from the sinner. The religious leaders criticized Jesus often for fellowshipping with sinners. Jesus was sent into the world by his Father and Holy Spirit, and now he is sending us into the world. We are called to preach the gospel to the sinner. The word of God will sanctify us while we are in this world.

Joh 17:17 Sanctify them through thy truth: thy word is truth.

Joh 17:18 As thou hast sent me into the world, even so have I also sent them into the world.

There are attitudes toward sin from the old nature that can hinder the work of sanctification in our lives. To change an attitude we first must realize we have one and then use the word to correct and prayer for help. A selfish attitude toward sin violates God's will and is an offensive act against God. We are not the moral compass; God's word is. Our attitude toward sin should be to put it away because it offends God and hinders us from running the race effectively. Differentiating between sins can be a hindrance because we will tend to ignore those sins we think are less sinful. Most believers overlook the list in (Eph 4:31) which deals with inward sins while believing others to be more grievous. Some of us find it easy to point out the faults of others while entirely blind to our own. How can I see to remove a speck out of my brother's eye when I have a log in my own (Luk 6:40-41)? Am I pointing the finger at my brother while ignoring my faults? Not understanding what true faith is, is a hindrance to holiness. All too often believers think that there is no action required to faith. Our works do not save us, but those with genuine living faith practice works of righteousness and holiness. We are Christ workmanship created to do good works that God ordained for us (Eph 2:8-10).

LESSON 8

Motivation of love

OBJECTIVE: Develop an understanding of the motivation of love.

THE ROYAL LAW
The Sovereign King's law

Jas 2:8   If ye fulfil **the royal law** according to the scripture, Thou shalt love thy neighbour as thyself, ye do well:

Mar 12:30   And thou shalt **love the Lord thy God** with all thy heart, and with all thy soul, and with all thy mind, and with all thy strength: this *is* the first commandment.

Mar 12:31   And the second *is* like, *namely* this, Thou shalt **love thy neighbour** as thyself. There is none other commandment greater than these.

God's love is the motivating force of all he does: God so loved that he gave (Joh 3:16). We have been redeemed by the blood of Jesus, and his love is shed abroad in our hearts and is meant to become the motivating force behind all of our actions (Rom 5:5). We cannot love our neighbor as ourselves without God's royal law of love working in us. We are commanded to love God and others, and God gives us his love to accomplish both. Because Jesus first loved us, we are motivated by his love to obey all that he commands. In loving one another as Christ loves us, we find our service to God in this new life.

> **Joh 15:12** This is my commandment, That ye **love one another, as I have loved you.**
>
> **Gal 5:13** For, brethren, ye have been called unto liberty; only *use* not liberty for an occasion to the flesh, but **by love serve one another.**
>
> **Gal 5:14** For all the law is fulfilled in one word, *even* in this; Thou shalt love thy neighbour as thyself.

THE LAW OF CHRIST

> **Gal 6:1** Brethren, if a man be overtaken in a fault, ye which are spiritual, **restore** such an one in the spirit of **meekness**; considering thyself, lest thou also be tempted.
>
> **Gal 6:2** Bear ye one another's burdens, and so fulfil **the law of Christ.**

- meekness—gentleness.

We can fulfill the royal law of Christ by loving others and helping them bear their burdens even as Christ helps us. As we consider others, it is important to not stand in judgment but to be a light to help them out of darkness. Our light cannot shine brightly in this dark world without being kindled by God's Holy love. If we judge, we must consider that we shall be judged by that same measure we use to judge others. He will work through us if love is our motivation. As members of the body of Christ, we are exhorted to care about those members who are weak and seek healing for their souls and bodies. As we reach out to minister, the Holy Spirit will manifest, working in and through us accomplishing God's purposes for his kingdom. We must learn to trust his leading. The Spirit of God led Jesus himself in all things, even to his temptation in the wilderness. With love for his Father and armed with the knowledge of the future, Christ fought the battle of faith using the sword of God's Word, and he won! Even so, can we for greater is he that is in us than the spirits that are in this world (1 Jn 4:4).

Any time we undertake to obey God, the enemy will come to steal the word planted in our heart. Many times Christians are unaware of what is taking place until it is too late. When we decide to love the temptation to do the opposite comes quickly to take away our resolve to live right. The enemy knows that it was God's love that brought down his kingdom and he will fight very hard to keep us from getting rooted and grounded in that love. He wills to divide the church but God wants us united, and love is the bond of perfection that unites us. We are not given a choice but a command to love, and if we love Jesus, we will love others.

Joh 14:15 If ye love me, keep my commandments.

Eph 3:14 For this cause I bow my knees unto the Father of our Lord Jesus Christ.

Eph 3:15 Of whom the whole family in heaven and earth is named.

Eph 3:16 That he would grant you, according to the riches of his glory, to be strengthened with might by his Spirit in the inner man;

Eph 3:17 That Christ may dwell in your hearts by faith; that ye, being **rooted and grounded in love**.

Eph 3:18 May be able **to comprehend** with all saints what *is* the breadth, and length, and depth, and height;

Eph 3:19 And **to know the love of Christ, which passeth knowledge**, that ye might **be filled with all the fulness of God**.

Eph 3:20 Now unto him that is able to do exceeding abundantly above all that we ask or think, according to the power that worketh in us.

Eph 3:21 Unto him *be* glory in the church by Christ Jesus throughout all ages, world without end. Amen.

- rooted—to root, become stable.
- grounded—to lay a basis for, to lay a foundation.
- comprehend—to take eagerly, seize, possess, apprehend.

1Jn 3:16 Hereby perceive we the **love *of God*,** because he laid down his life for us: and we ought to lay down *our* lives for the brethren.

1Jn 3:17 But whoso hath this world's good, and seeth his brother have need, and shutteth up his **bowels *of compassion*** from him, how dwelleth the love of God in him?

1Jn 3:18 My little children, **let us not love in word, neither in tongue; but in deed and in truth.**

Paul prayed that we would be rooted and grounded in love. After living this earthly life in the old man who is selfish by nature, it is a drastic change for God's will to be the center of our lives. However, the new man with the new love nature has God's love, and this love is what motivates him to do what he can for his brother. Paul prayed that we may become stable in walking out God's love in our daily life and that we would be able to take eagerly; to possess the breadth, length, depth, and height and perceive the love of Christ. If Christ laid down his life for us because of such love, then we ought to do the same for each other. If we desire to serve Jesus, this transformational love is necessary for all ministry to the saints.

DWELL IN GOD'S LOVE

1Jn 4:15 Whosoever shall confess that Jesus is the Son of God, God dwelleth in him, and he in God.

1Jn 4:16 And we have **known and believed the love** that God hath to us. **God is love**; and he that **dwelleth in love dwelleth in God, and God in him.**

1Jn 4:17 Herein is our love made perfect, that we may have boldness in the day of judgment: because as he is, so are we in this world.

Rom 5:5 And hope maketh not ashamed; because **the love of God is shed abroad in our hearts by the Holy Ghost** which is given unto us.

The precious Holy Spirit is God, and God is love. The Holy Spirit dwells within each believer loving us and loving others through us. He is our comforter and our wise counselor, and he is the power of God who helps us. God's selfless love suffers rejection and persecution yet continues to love in a magnitude that is unfathomable. His Son was nailed to a tree despising the shame, yet stayed the course to make way for our glorification. Though he was suffering untold misery, Jesus loved as he looked down from the cross and asked his Father to forgive the ones who caused him this pain. It was love that held our Savior to the cross and faith that a generation to come would dwell with him and his Father. Love, a fruit of the Holy Spirit is the evidence to others that one belongs to Christ. Jesus said the world would know that we are his disciples by our love (Joh 17). God's love is shed abroad in the heart of the believer.

Joh 15:7   If ye abide in me, and my words abide in you, ye shall ask what ye will, and it shall be done unto you.

Joh 15:8   Herein is my Father glorified, that ye bear much fruit; so shall ye be my disciples.

Joh 15:9   As the Father hath loved me, so have I loved you: continue ye in my love.

Joh 15:10   **If ye keep my commandments, ye shall abide in my love;** even as I have kept my Father's commandments, and abide in his love.

Joh 15:11   These things have I spoken unto you, that **my joy** might remain in you, and *that* your joy might be full.

Joh 15:12   **This is my commandment, That ye love one another, as I have loved you.**

MOVE WITH COMPASSION

- moved with compassion—to have the bowels yearn, that is feel sympathy, pity.

Mat 14:14   And Jesus went forth, and saw a great multitude, and was **moved with compassion** toward them, and he healed their sick.

Mat 9:35   And Jesus went about all the cities and villages, teaching in their synagogues, and preaching the gospel of the kingdom, and healing every sickness and every disease among the people.

Mat 9:36   **But when he saw the multitudes, he was moved with compassion** on them, because they fainted, and were scattered abroad, as sheep having no shepherd.

Mat 9:37   Then saith he unto his disciples, The harvest truly *is* plenteous, but the labourers *are* few;

Mat 9:38   **Pray ye therefore** the Lord of the harvest, that he will send forth labourers into his harvest.

Jesus saw the people like sheep without a shepherd to lead them, and he moved with compassion. The crowds pressed in to hear Jesus and receive healing of their diseases. The multitudes followed him even to the point of going without food for days, and Jesus fed them. Jesus compassion moved him to heal every sickness and every disease among the people, and it also led him to pray and urge others to pray for more laborers to help with the Harvest. God does not want any to perish but have eternal life through Jesus.

The Pharisees and Sadducees cared not about the people's welfare and thought themselves more holy. They did not want to tarnish their reputations by being seen with a sinner. Instead of having compassion they laid heavy burdens upon the people they would not even bear (Mat 23:4).

Col 3:12   **Put on** therefore, as the elect of God, holy and beloved, **bowels of mercies**, kindness, humbleness of mind, meekness, longsuffering;

Col 3:13   Forbearing one another, and forgiving one another, if any man have a quarrel against any: even as Christ forgave you, so also *do* ye.

THE BOND OF PERFECTION

Col 3:14   And above all these things *put on* charity, which is the **bond of perfectness.**

Col 3:15   And let the peace of God rule in your hearts, to the which also ye are called.

Mat 5:43   Ye have heard that it hath been said, Thou shalt love thy neighbour, and hate thine enemy.

Mat 5:44   But I say unto you, **Love your enemies**, bless them that curse you, do good to them that hate you, and pray for them which despitefully use you, and persecute you;

Mat 5:45   That ye may be the children of your Father which is in heaven: for he maketh his sun to rise on the evil and on the good, and sendeth rain on the just and on the unjust.

Mat 5:46 For if ye love them which love you, what reward have ye? do not even the publicans the same?

Mat 5:47 And if ye salute your brethren only, what do ye more *than others?* do not even the publicans so?

Mat 5:48 Be ye therefore perfect, even as your Father which is in heaven is perfect.

God's perfect love extends beyond the boundaries of family and friends and envelopes its enemy. As Jesus enemies crucified him, he asked his Father to forgive them for they didn't know what they were doing. This is the kind of love the Holy Ghost sheds abroad in our hearts. Those men did not understand that they were pawns in the devil's hands. They did not realize they were crucifying the very Son of God sent to save the world. Jesus perfect love cast out fear in the face of the enemy and extends forgiveness for suffered wrongs. Imagine the effect of Jesus merciful heart toward his persecutors even to the end. One of the two thieves called him Lord and asked Christ to remember him when he came into his kingdom. Jesus told the thief that he would be with him that day in Paradise. The thief, as Jesus promised, found himself in Abrahams bosom instead of the fires of hell. All who believe in Jesus may have boldness in the day of judgment for God's perfect love has saved us. We do not have to fear God's wrath because Christ paid the wages of our sins on the cross.

1Jn 4:16 And we have known and believed the love that God hath to us. God is love; and he that dwelleth in love dwelleth in God, and God in him.

1Jn 4:17 Herein is our love made perfect, that we may have boldness in the day of judgment: because as he is, so are we in this world.

1Jn 4:18 **There is no fear in love;** but **perfect love casteth out fear**: because fear hath torment. He that feareth is not made perfect in love.

1Jn 4:19 We love him, because he first loved us.

1Jn 4:20 If a man say, I love God, and hateth his brother, he is a liar: for he that loveth not his brother whom he hath seen, how can he love God whom he hath not seen?

Col 3:12 Put on therefore, as the elect of God, holy and beloved, bowels of mercies, kindness, humbleness of mind, meekness, longsuffering;

Col 3:13 Forbearing one another, and forgiving one another, if any man have a quarrel against any: even as Christ forgave you, so also *do* ye.

Col 3:14 And above all these things *put on* **charity, which is the bond of perfectness.**

1Co 13:1 Though I speak with the tongues of men and of angels, and have not charity, I am become *as* sounding brass, or a tinkling cymbal.

1Co 13:2 And though I have *the gift of* prophecy, and understand all mysteries, and all knowledge; and though I have all faith, so that I could remove mountains, and have not charity, I am nothing.

1Co 13:3 And though I bestow all my goods to feed *the poor*, and though I give my body to be burned, and have not charity, it profiteth me nothing.

1Co 13:4   Charity suffereth long, *and* is kind; charity envieth not; charity vaunteth not itself, is not puffed up.

1Co 13:5   Doth not behave itself unseemly, seeketh not her own, is not easily provoked, thinketh no evil;

1Co 13:6   Rejoiceth not in iniquity, but rejoiceth in the truth;

1Co 13:7   Beareth all things, believeth all things, hopeth all things, endureth all things.

1Co 13:8   **Charity never faileth:** but whether *there be* prophecies, they shall fail; whether *there be* tongues, they shall cease; whether *there be* knowledge, it shall vanish away.

2Co 2:10   To whom ye forgive any thing, I forgive also: for if I forgave any thing, to whom I forgave it, for your sakes **forgave I it in the person of Christ;**

2Co 2:11   Lest Satan should get an advantage of us: for we are not ignorant of his devices.

If we do not forgive others, our adversary takes advantage of the situation to cause havoc and destruction in our relationships. Refusing to will produce a root of bitterness that will defile the heart and the atmosphere around us, adversely affecting ourselves and others because of our words or actions. Instead of words of grace seasoned with salt, our mouth will spew out words of envy and strife and division. Bitterness will cause us to be temperamental and look to blame others for the emotions we are feeling, and it causes us to justify our ungodly actions. The result is that we become an accuser of the brethren, which is a character trait of Satan. When we forgive, we love and cover a multitude of sins, which is a character trait of Christ. When we believe and obey his command to love others, we are protecting our own heart with the breastplate of faith and love. We must make a conscious choice to forgive, in obedience to God's commandments. If we do not forgive we are not obeying God's commandments, and we leave our own heart unprotected and vulnerable to the devil's wiles. We are to walk in wisdom toward believers and unbelievers, bearing witness to the truth of the gospel of peace.

As you can see, we have many things to lay on God's altar as we present ourselves to him in prayer and service. Let us examine our hearts in the light of God's word for proper motivation in our daily relationships and the ministry. If we are to walk in God's ways, we must forget the old ways and put on bowels of mercy toward others and forgive and forbear with them in compassion. Applying this foundational truth is vital in the transformation process into Christ image. May the Lord give us his heart for others and may we not desire vain glory but endeavor to serve him with a pure heart. We can and will do this with the help of our precious companion, Holy Spirit, who dwells in us.

LESSON 9

Humility in Action

OBJECTIVE: Develop and demonstrate an understanding of the value of humility.

HUMILITY IS AN ATTRIBUTE OF LOVE

Humility is the opposite of pride and is an attribute of love. Love does not brag or boast nor does it inflate the ego and make one proud, but is humble. To humble ourselves under the mighty hand of God is to admit our weaknesses before him to obtain mercy and find grace to help in time of need Heb 4:14-16.

> 1Co 13:4 Charity suffereth long, *and* is kind; charity envieth not; charity **vaunteth not itself, is not puffed up.**

- vaunteth—braggart, to boast.

- puffed up—to inflate, to make proud.

Pro 16:18 **Pride** goeth before destruction, and an haughty spirit before a fall.

Pro 16:19 **Better it is to be of an humble spirit with the lowly,** than to divide the spoil with the proud.

Isa 57:15 For thus saith the high and lofty One that inhabiteth eternity, whose name is Holy; I dwell in the high and holy place, with him also that is of **a contrite and humble spirit, to revive** the spirit of the humble, and to revive the heart of the contrite ones.

- God revives the spirit of the humble and the heart of the contrite ones.

A contrite (crushed) heart and humble spirit express feelings of remorse and brokenness over their sins. The woman with the alabaster box of ointment who anointed Jesus was very contrite as she came broken before him weeping, kissing his feet, washing them with her tears, anointing them and wiping them with her hair. Such expression of love and gratitude for Christ was extravagant and men like Simon the Pharisee would think excessive. When the alabaster box is broken to pour out the ointment, its fragrance filled the air.

When we are broken before the Lord as this woman and poured out, our worship will ascend before him as a sweet smelling fragrance, even extravagant love. She came broken and in faith and was accepted and her sins forgiven.

Luk 7:36 And one of the Pharisees desired him that he would eat with him. And he went into the Pharisee's house, and sat down to meat.

Luk 7:37 And, behold, a woman in the city, which was a sinner, when she knew that Jesus sat at meat in the Pharisee's house, brought an alabaster box of ointment.

Luk 7:38 And stood at his feet behind him weeping, and began to wash his feet with tears, and did wipe them with the hairs of her head, and kissed his feet, and anointed them with the ointment.

Luk 7:39 Now when the Pharisee which had bidden him saw it, he spake within himself, saying, This man, if he were a prophet, would have known who and what manner of woman this is that toucheth him: for she is a sinner.

Luk 7:40 And Jesus answering said unto him, Simon, I have somewhat to say unto thee. And he saith, Master, say on.

Luk 7:41 There was a certain creditor which had two debtors: the one owed five hundred pence, and the other fifty.

Luk 7:42 And when they had nothing to pay, he frankly forgave them both. Tell me therefore, which of them will love him most?

Luk 7:43 Simon answered and said, I suppose that he, to whom he forgave most. And he said unto him, Thou hast rightly judged.

Luk 7:44 And he turned to the woman, and said unto Simon, Seest thou this woman? I entered into thine house, thou gavest me no water for my feet: but she hath washed my feet with tears, and wiped them with the hairs of her head.

Luk 7:45 Thou gavest me no kiss: but this woman since the time I came in hath not ceased to kiss my feet.

Luk 7:46 My head with oil thou didst not anoint: but this woman hath anointed my feet with ointment.

Luk 7:47 Wherefore I say unto thee, Her sins, which are many, are forgiven; for she loved much: but to whom little is forgiven, the same loveth little.

Luk 7:48 And he said unto her, Thy sins are forgiven.

Luk 7:49 And they that sat at meat with him began to say within themselves, Who is this that forgiveth sins also?

Luk 7:50 And he said to the woman, **Thy faith hath saved thee;** go in peace.

The very Messiah of the scripture that was prophesied to come was sitting there before him, and he did not offer Jesus even the common hospitalities provided guests. This Pharisee would not dream of stooping to the level of letting a sinner touch him, especially one such as this woman. Simon reasoned that if Jesus were a true prophet he would not allow this woman to defile him. In his own eyes, Simon thought himself better. He did not understand what was occurring right before his eyes, but he was watching true humility in action.

THE HUMBLE ARE EXALTED

A humble person is not a fearful person but one who believes and trust God in all things. He does not exalt himself but he will be the one God exalts. Jesus tells a parable which demonstrates humility and exaltation.

Luk 14:7 And he put forth a parable to those which were bidden, when he marked how they chose out the chief rooms; saying unto them.

Luk 14:8 When thou art bidden of any *man* to a wedding, sit not down in the highest room; lest a more honourable man than thou be bidden of him;

Luk 14:9 And he that bade thee and him come and say to thee, Give this man place; and thou begin with shame to take the lowest room.

Luk 14:10 But when thou art bidden, go and sit down in the lowest room; that when he that bade thee cometh, he may say unto thee, Friend, go up higher: then shalt thou have worship in the presence of them that sit at meat with thee.

Luk 14:11 For whosoever exalteth himself shall be abased; and he that humbleth himself shall be exalted.

Many of the religious leaders of Jesus time were motivated by lust for power, fear of man, or pride instead of a genuine concern for God's will or love of God's people. They were prideful, seeing themselves as better, trusting in their self-righteousness. In (Mat 5:20) Jesus said unless our righteousness exceeds that of the scribes and Pharisees we will not enter the kingdom of heaven. The rulers held that keeping the law and certain traditions made them righteous and worthy of blessing. God said that he that humbles himself would be justified. Jesus told a parable of two men in the temple praying. One was a Pharisee, and the other was a publican who is a tax collector. The tax collector, convicted of his sins could not even lift his head but humbled himself before God asking for mercy. The Pharisee trusted in himself and thanked God that he wasn't a sinner like other men, even the publican praying near him. He refused to examine the condition of his own heart which was full of pride and did not humble himself before God. Jesus said the one who was contrite and cried out for mercy confessing his sins was the one that was made right with God.

Luk 18:9 And he spake this parable unto certain which **trusted in themselves** that they were righteous, and despised others:

Luk 18:10 Two men went up into the temple to pray; the one a Pharisee, and the other a publican.

Luk 18:11 The Pharisee stood and prayed thus with himself, **God, I thank thee, that I am not as other men** *are,* extortioners, unjust, adulterers, or even as this publican.

Luk 18:12 I fast twice in the week, I give tithes of all that I possess.

Luk 18:13 And the publican, standing afar off, would not lift up so much as *his* eyes unto heaven, but smote upon his breast, saying, **God be merciful to me a sinner.**

Luk 18:14 I tell you, this man went down to his house justified *rather* than the other: for every one that exalteth himself shall be abased; and he that humbleth himself shall be exalted.

The story of David the lowly shepherd boy is a classic example of God resisting the proud and exalting the humble (1Sam 16). God had rejected Saul from being king and sent Samuel to anoint one of the sons of Jesse to be king. At one time Saul was little in his own eyes but he came to care more about the adulation of the people then obeying God. Samuel, after inviting Jesse and his sons to come to his sacrifice, prepared to anoint one of the seven sons of Jesse as king. Each son was presented before him one at a time beginning at the eldest.

Surely this was the Lord's anointed Samuel thought as he looked at the eldest, but the Lord rejected him and his six brothers with him. God told Samuel not to look at the outward appearance for we do not see the way God sees, for God sees the heart. After inquiring whether Jesse had any more sons, David was sent for and anointed King of Israel. He walked humbly with his God; therefore God exalted him. Unlike his older brothers, he was not even invited to the sacrifice by his father. Jesse did not even fathom his youngest son as being chosen by God, yet God looked into the heart and found who was worthy of being King.

> 1Sa 16:6   And it came to pass, when they were come, that he looked on Eliab, and said, Surely the LORD'S anointed *is* before him.

> 1Sa 16:7   But the LORD said unto Samuel, Look not on his countenance, or on the height of his stature; because I have refused him: for *the LORD seeth* not as man seeth; **for man looketh on the outward appearance, but the LORD looketh on the heart.**

Like God looks at the heart, a humble man strives to look beyond the flesh to know the person. We are not to see any man after the flesh any longer but after the spirit (2Co 5:16). Humility in the disciple causes him to see the value in each person knowing all are loved by God equally. A humble person does not see himself as above others and therefore does not need to protect his reputation. He understands that each is important to God's purpose and plan which helps keep us grounded. We will not feel threatened by others in ministry but joyfully give them space to grow in their calling. It is not always easy to take a back seat so others can be exalted, but true humility submits to God's wisdom.

WISDOM AND HONOR GIVEN TO THE HUMBLE

The humble understand the value of and receive the sound wisdom that is laid up for the righteous.

Pro 11:2 *When* pride cometh, then cometh shame: but with **the lowly** is **wisdom.**

Pro 15:33 The fear of the LORD is the **instruction of wisdom;** and **before honour is humility.**

Pro 18:12 Before destruction the heart of man is haughty, and **before honour** *is* **humility.**

Pro 22:4 **By humility** *and* the fear of the LORD *are* riches, and **honour,** and life.

As we humble ourselves before God and receive his wisdom by the revelation of the Holy Ghost, we are transformed from glory to glory (honor to honor) into the image of Christ. The more we grow in Christ, the more Christ increases, and we decrease. Christ who is the greatest of all men is meek (gentle) and lowly (humble) in heart (Mat 11:29). Humility was a way of life with Jesus, and so it should be for the believer.

Pro 29:23 A man's pride shall bring him low: but **honour shall uphold the humble in spirit.**

- honor—splendor, glorious.

- uphold—sustain, help.

2Co 12:9 And he said unto me, My grace is sufficient for thee: for my strength is made perfect in weakness. Most gladly therefore will I rather glory in my infirmities, that the power of Christ may rest upon me.

2Co 12:10 Therefore I take pleasure in infirmities, in reproaches, in necessities, in persecutions, in distresses for Christ's sake: for when I am weak, then am I strong.

Paul found that no matter what he faced for Christ sake there would be strength provided by God's all-sufficient grace. He looked forward to experiencing the glory of God's strength working in him. That is why he said he would rather glory in his infirmities so the power of Christ would rest upon him. Confessing our weaknesses before God is humbling ourselves before him that we might receive from his sufficiency perfecting his strength in us. A humble man can do all things through Christ because he understands that it is Christ who is providing and not himself. Paul knew how to live with little or with much through finding his sufficiency in God.

CHRISTLIKE HUMILITY

Col 3:12 Put on therefore, as the elect of God, holy and beloved, bowels of mercies, kindness, **humbleness of mind,** meekness, longsuffering;

1Pe 5:5 Likewise, ye younger, submit yourselves unto the elder. Yea, all *of you* be subject one to another, and **be clothed with humility: for God resisteth the proud, and giveth grace to the humble.**

Mic 6:8 He hath shewed thee, O man, what *is* good; and what doth the LORD require of thee, but to do justly, and to love mercy, and **to walk humbly** with thy God?

Mat 11:29 Take my yoke upon you, and **learn of me; for I am meek and lowly in heart:** and ye shall find rest unto your souls.

We clothe ourselves with humility by seeing Christ revealed in the scriptures and being transformed supernaturally by the power of that word into that same image of humility. We are to let the mind of Christ be in us with all humility and submission, and

God will exalt us in due time as he exalted his son. Of course, we shall never be above our Lord and Savior, but we are to have this like-mindedness of Christ. As Christ humbled himself to serve his Father, we are to humble ourselves to serve God and one another. Our perspective toward one another is an essential aspect of our call for we must learn to work with others together for the common goal of God's purpose. Transformation in humility is learning to rest in God's leadership.

Php 2:3 *Let* nothing *be done* through strife or vainglory; but **in lowliness of mind let each esteem other better than themselves.**

Php 2:4 Look not every man on his own things, but every man also on the things of others.

Php 2:5 **Let this mind be in you, which was also in Christ Jesus:**

Php 2:6 Who, being in the form of God, thought it not robbery to be equal with God:

Php 2:7 But made himself of no reputation, and **took upon him the form of a servant,** and was made in the likeness of men:

Php 2:8 And being found in fashion as a man, **he humbled himself,** and became obedient unto death, even the death of the cross.

Php 2:9 **Wherefore God also hath highly exalted him,** and given him a name which is above every name:

Php 2:10 That at the name of Jesus every knee should bow, of *things* in heaven, and *things* in earth, and *things* under the earth;

Php 2:11   And *that* every tongue should confess that Jesus Christ *is* Lord, to the glory of God the Father.

Mat 23:11   But he that is greatest among you shall be your servant.

Mat 23:12   And whosoever shall exalt himself shall be abased; and **he that shall humble himself shall be exalted.**

Joh 12:42   Nevertheless among the chief rulers also many believed on him; but because of the Pharisees they did not confess *him*, lest they should be put out of the synagogue:

Joh 12:43   For they loved the praise of men more than the praise of God.

The greatest act of humility was Jesus becoming a servant and being obedient to his father unto death to serve all humanity. As a result, he is exalted far above all; King of kings and Lord of lords. Jesus told the disciples that the greatest among us is the servant (Mat 23:11-12). The virtue of humility cares nothing about receiving praise from men but wants the honor that comes from God alone. It is liberating for there is no pressure to look good in the eyes of any but God. Humility frees us from pride as we look at others with value and understand that we too are weak. Like Paul, we can say, "by the grace of God I am what I am" (1 Co 15:10).

GRACE IS GIVEN TO THE HUMBLE

Humility should be the clothing of every Christian for God gives grace to the humble.

1Pe 5:5   Likewise, ye **younger, submit yourselves unto the elder.** Yea, all *of you* **be subject one to another,** and **be clothed with humility**: for God resisteth the proud, and **giveth grace to the humble.**

1Pe 5:6 **Humble yourselves** therefore under the mighty hand of God, that he may exalt you in due time:

- humility—modesty, lowliness of mind.
- resisteth—oppose, set himself against.

God's will is for us to submit to him in all things including his established authority of leadership that governs the Church on earth. The younger is to submit to the elder. The meaning of the word younger in this sentence in (1Pet 5) is not only about age but also about those who are newly regenerate in the Lord. They are babes in Christ until trained by the word of God. It is essential for them to learn to submit to the elders and drink in the milk of the word of God. All believers are to submit to one another as we recognize the authority of the Spirit of God working in them. In this we are humbling ourselves under God's hand, trusting his wisdom in all things; even working through others. We must examine what is taught by others in the light of God's word and yield to the truth with a spirit of humility. If the teaching is an error, the Spirit of truth will discern it.

It is understandable that those called to minister desire to fulfill their calling; however, we must learn humility and God will exalt us in his time. Then we may walk in the authority of God's Kingdom in that calling. When we submit to God's authority in others, his authority and power will be manifest through us. If we resist God's will regarding submission, it is because of pride. God opposes the proud but gives grace to the humble.

LESSON 10

The Abundant Life

OBJECTIVE: **Develop and demonstrate an understanding of how to live the abundant life.**

TO KNOW GOD

Joh 10:10   The thief cometh not, but for to steal, and to kill, and to destroy: I am come that they might have **life,** and that they might have *it* **more abundantly**.

- more abundantly—superior in quality or superabundant in quantity; beyond measure

Joh 14:6   Jesus saith unto him, I am the way, the truth, and **the life**: no man cometh unto the Father, but by me.

Joh 14:7   If ye had known me, ye should have known my Father also: and from henceforth ye know him, and have seen him.

Mat 6:25   Therefore I say unto you, **Take no thought for your life, what ye shall eat, or what ye shall drink; nor yet for your body,** what ye shall put on. **Is not the life more than meat,** and the body than raiment?

The abundant life is more than just having shelter, food, and clothing. The abundance of life is the superior life of the new man in Christ living from the wealth of the kingdom of God. We are resurrected with a new life so that we might know and serve the living God. We will not find satisfaction in anything on this earth because our need for the spiritual is much greater than our need for the physical. Jesus said what good will it do to gain the whole world and lose your soul (Mat 16:26).

Joh 17:3   And this is **life eternal, that they might know thee** the only true God, and Jesus Christ, whom thou hast sent.

We cannot begin to know and live an abundant life without the knowledge of the Son of God. He is Life! If we do not know the Son of God, we cannot know the Father. The Father has chosen that in his Son we should be blessed and have everlasting life. He has blessed us with all spiritual blessings in heavenly places and given us the honor of being sons who sit with him in the heavens (Eph 1). His plan from the foundation of the world is that we should be adopted as his children by Jesus Christ. The abundant life is that heavenly kingdom family life as children of God. As our Father, he will provide our needs as we seek first his kingdom and his righteousness. When we believe his word and obey, we are giving access to our lives for God to shed upon us the blessings and power of his kingdom. Jesus preached the gospel of the kingdom of God, and he brought the authority of that kingdom into the earth to give life. Like Jesus, we too can bring the kingdom of God into our lives and the lives of others. In (Mat 12:28) Jesus said that if he cast out the devils by the Spirit of God, then the kingdom of God has come to you. When he ministered to the poor, the sick, the possessed, the lame, the blind, to all oppressed by the devil, he set them free by the power of the Holy Spirit, the power of God's kingdom. We bring the power of God's kingdom to earth through the preaching of the gospel under the unction of the Holy Spirit. In Christ Jesus, we have a new identity and are seated with him in the place of rulership above all principality and powers (Eph 1:21,22; Eph 2:6). It is imperative that we not only believe in our new identity but walk in the light of this revelation in communication with God. Should we not view life from the spiritual perspective of being in him? Those who dwell in Jesus are given all spiritual blessings from the Father. The greatest and most abundant life blessing is to know (experience) God our Father and his Son. Then through that communion, the authority of his kingdom will be demonstrated on earth through us, as it was through Jesus, to bring others into that same fellowship. The abundant life is a superior quality of life than the old, being far beyond its measure. The emphasis of the early church was a new quality of life for the present, not just reserved for the future as unfortunately many believe. We have an invitation, so come boldly into the throne room and commune with God. Now, we are alive to God and he to us!

ADOPTION

It is abundance of life knowing and living like we belong and are accepted as part of God's family through adoption. All the spiritual blessings in the heavenly places belong to us who are in Christ. His plan for us is for good to give us a future far beyond anything we could dream of. To know that we are blessed, chosen, predestined to adoption, accepted in his beloved and redeemed by the precious blood is the foundation for receiving the promises of his kingdom. Through Christ we receive all things for he has made us joint heirs with him. We have been invited to partake from his table for we are forgiven, accepted, graced with his high favor, chosen in Christ and given all spiritual blessings in the heavenly places where we now sit. Perspective from the higher realm is the pleasure of God's great plan for man. He gives us light that we might see all he has placed within and find joy in fellowshipping with him.

Eph 1:3 Blessed *be* the God and Father of our Lord Jesus Christ, who hath **blessed us with all spiritual blessings** in heavenly *places* in Christ:

Eph 1:4 According as he hath **chosen us in him** before the foundation of the world, that we should be holy and without blame before him in love.

Eph 1:5 Having **predestinated us unto the adoption of children** by Jesus Christ to himself, according to the good pleasure of his will.

Eph 1:6 To the praise of the glory of his grace, wherein he hath made us **accepted** in the beloved.

Eph 1:7 In whom we have **redemption** through his blood, the forgiveness of sins, according to the riches of his grace;

Eph 1:8 And hath raised *us* up together, and made *us* sit together in heavenly *places* in Christ Jesus:

Rom 8:15 For ye have not received **the spirit of bondage again to fear; but ye have received the Spirit of adoption, whereby we cry, Abba, Father.**

Rom 8:16 The Spirit itself beareth witness with our spirit, that we are the children of God:

Rom 8:17   And **if children, then heirs; heirs of God, and joint-heirs with Christ;** if so be that we suffer with *him,* that we may be also glorified together.

Rom 8:18   For I reckon that the sufferings of this present time *are* not worthy *to be compared* with **the glory which shall be revealed in us.**

CHILDREN OF LIGHT

Joh 1:4   In him was life; and the **life was the light** of men.

Joh 8:12   Then spake Jesus again unto them, saying, **I am the light of the world:** he that followeth me shall not walk in darkness, but shall have the **light of life.**

Eph 5:8   For ye were sometimes darkness, but **now** *are ye* **light in the Lord:** walk as children of light:

1Jn 1:1   That which was from the beginning, which we have heard, which we have seen with our eyes, which we have looked upon, and our hands have handled, of the Word of life;

1Jn 1:2   (For **the life was manifested**, and we have seen *it,* and bear witness, and shew unto you that **eternal life,** which was with the Father, and was manifested unto us;)

1Jn 1:3   That which we have seen and heard declare we unto you, that ye also may have fellowship with us: and truly our **fellowship** *is* **with the Father, and with his Son Jesus Christ.**

1Jn 1:4 And these things write we unto you, **that your joy may be full.**

1Jn 1:5 This then is the message which we have heard of him, and declare unto you, that **God is light,** and in him is no darkness at all.

1Jn 1:6 If we say that we have fellowship with him, and walk in darkness, we lie, and do not the truth:

1Jn 1:7 But **if we walk in the light, as he is in the light, we have fellowship one with another**, and the blood of Jesus Christ his Son cleanseth us from all sin.

Psa 36:9 For with thee is the fountain of life: **in thy light shall we see light.**

- fellowship—partnership, participation, to communicate

Psa 16:11 Thou wilt shew me the path of life: in thy presence *is* fulness of joy; at thy right hand *there are* pleasures for evermore.

The very presence of God causes joy in those who are graced by him. Man was created for fellowship with God and walked in the light of God's glory communing with him in the Garden of Eden on God's holy Mount. When Adam and Eve sinned, they hid from the presence of God because of their nakedness, and they were afraid (Gen 3:8-10). Men have been hiding from God ever since. We who believe in Jesus, however, come boldly into God's presence through our Great High Priest Jesus. We are not naked and afraid because we are clothed with Christ. There is no condemnation to those who are in Christ Jesus. Being clothed with his righteousness we have confidence with God and enter the Holy Mountain of Zion in heavenly Jerusalem to fellowship with him (Heb 12:22-24).

Gen 3:8 And they heard the voice of the LORD God walking in the garden in the cool of the day: and Adam and his wife **hid themselves from the presence of the LORD God** amongst the trees of the garden.

Adam and Eve's disobedience caused the glory of the Lord to depart from their temples, and they were naked. They were no longer in a holy and pure state and were ashamed, so they covered themselves and hid from God. With the sin and shame came the spirit of fear and bondage and men began to run and hide from God, although God sees and knows all. When Adam walked with God in the light, he was free from all the effects of the kingdom of darkness and blessed with God's Kingdom light. Jesus came to restore to us our freedom and relationship with God. Praise Jesus Holy Name!

2Co 3:17 Now the Lord is that Spirit: and **where the Spirit of the Lord *is*, there *is* liberty.**

2Co 3:18 But we all, with open face beholding as in a glass the glory of the Lord, are **changed into the same image from glory to glory,** *even* as by the Spirit of the Lord.

We who have the Spirit of God in us are the light of the world. Adam and Eve knew only the light of God's glory until they lost their glory. We are invited to come and grow from glory to glory as we are transformed into Christ likeness through faith in his word. Yes, we are called to glory and virtue and made to partake of his divine nature which we are to demonstrate to the world.

Mat 5:14 Ye are the light of the world. A city that is set on an hill cannot be hid.

Mat 5:15   Neither do men light a candle, and put it under a bushel, but on a candlestick; and it giveth light unto all that are in the house.

Mat 5:16   **Let your light so shine before men,** that they may see your good works, and glorify your Father which is in heaven.

2Pe 1:3   According as his divine power hath given unto us all things that *pertain* unto **life and godliness, through the knowledge of him that hath called us to glory and virtue:**

2Pe 1:4   Whereby are given unto us exceeding great and precious **promises**: that by these ye might be **partakers of the divine nature**, having escaped the corruption that is in the world through lust.

Phm 1:6 That the communication of thy faith may become effectual by the acknowledging of every good thing which is in you in Christ Jesus.

As we confess the precious promises of God regarding all Christ has graced us with, our faith is made effectual. The abundant life is in the communication of the great and precious promises of God's word. The divine nature will overtake and destroy all that opposes it in our hearts as we believe and confess what Christ Jesus has accomplished for us and in us. We partake of the divine nature through faith in his word and fellowship in the Spirit where we dwell in his love and walk in his light. The life manifested to his disciples, and they fellowshipped with him in the flesh and believed in him. John wanted us to know that fellowshipping in the light with God fills one with joy. We are the light of the world which expels the darkness and draws men to Christ through the preaching of the cross. God's light will shine through us to accomplish this as we find our joy drawing near to him.

GIVEN HIS GLORY

- glory—dignity, honor, praise, worship.

In (Joh 17:5) Jesus prayed that he would be restored the glory (dignity) that he shared with the Father before he came to earth. His fellowship with the Father was in the oneness of the Holy Spirit though **he was in the flesh, and his glory was veiled by it**. The disciples got a glimpse of Christ glory on the Mount of Transfiguration (Mat 17:2). When Jesus was resurrected the glory he shared with the Father was restored, only now manifested in a man's frame (Rev 1:13-16). Jesus gave us his glory through the Holy Spirit that we could become one with him, and the Father and one another. The Holy Spirit sent to dwell within has the fullness of **God's Shekinah glory, and he is veiled by our flesh**. His glory and divine power have given us everything we need to live an abundant life of godliness. As he led and empowered Jesus, he will do the same for us.

Mat 17:1   And after six days Jesus taketh Peter, James, and John his brother, and bringeth them up into an high mountain apart.

Mat 17:2   And was **transfigured before them: and his face did shine as the sun, and his raiment was white as the light.**

Joh 17:5   And now, O Father, glorify thou me with thine own self with **the glory which I had with thee before the world was.**

Joh 17:21   That they all may be one; as thou, Father, *art* in me, and I in thee, that they also may be one in us: that the world may believe that thou hast sent me.

Joh 17:22   And **the glory which thou gavest me I have given them; that they may be one, even as we are one:**

Joh 17:23   **I in them, and thou in me, that they may be made perfect in one;** and that the world may know that thou hast sent me, and hast loved them, as thou hast loved me.

2Co 4:6   For God, who commanded the light to shine out of darkness, hath shined in our hearts, to *give* the **light of the knowledge of the glory of God in the face of Jesus Christ.**

2Co 4:7   But we have this **treasure in earthen vessels,** that the excellency of the power may be of God, and not of us.

Glory in the Hebrew conveys a weight, an exceeding splendor which is what the disciples saw in Christ. His face shined like the sun, and his clothing was white as light. God's light shined into our hearts that we might see his glory in the face of his son Jesus Christ. Paul calls this glory that we have received from Jesus a treasure in earthen vessels. We have been translated out of the kingdom of darkness and translated into the kingdom of God's son. It is a kingdom of light. When we walk in the pure light of life, we are walking a life of glory and dignity bringing honor to our God.

Jesus gave us his glory, and one day we shall be clothed with the fullness of that beauty and manifested to all as the Sons of God (2Th 1:10). All creation is longing for the day when the inheritance of the sons of God will be evident at the Revelation of Christ. All creation also has the hope of deliverance from corruption (Ro 8:18-23).

1Ch 16:27   **Glory and honour** *are* **in his presence;** strength and gladness *are* in his place.

The abundant life is found in oneness with the Son of God, the Father, the Holy Spirit, and our brethren; dwelling in love and being filled with all his fullness (Eph 3:19). We are alive to God and have a relationship with him, and without him, we have no life. Think about it: God permeating every facet of our being with his life. That is why Paul pressed on to know him in every way he possibly could, even in his sufferings. Paul fellowshipped with Christ and experienced Christ life living in and through him. He learned how to be content while going through trials by submitting to God — trusting in God's goodness and his faithfulness in times of lack and in times of abundance results in contentment in either condition. Realizing his weakness in the situations he encountered, Paul found that God's grace was sufficient for life in every need. As we learn to trust God in every trial our faith is being perfected (1 Pet 1:7). The abundant life is a walk of love, hope, faith, and courage during trials and opposition from men and satanic forces. Faith working by the love of God gave the disciples the ability to endure every temptation and win the victory. Knowing Christ intimately gave them the ability to offer forgiveness to those who persecuted them even as Christ forgave. They showed love and generosity, walked in peace and exhibited godliness in character which gave integrity to their message.

> 2Co 12:9   And he said unto me, **My grace is sufficient for thee: for my strength is made perfect in weakness.** Most gladly therefore will I rather glory in my infirmities, that the power of Christ may rest upon me.

> 2Co 12:10   Therefore I take pleasure in infirmities, in reproaches, in necessities, in persecutions, in distresses for Christ's sake: for **when I am weak, then am I strong.**

2Ti 4:6   For I am now ready to be offered, and the time of my departure is at hand.

2Ti 4:7   I have fought a good fight, I have finished *my* course, I have kept the faith:

2Ti 4:8   Henceforth there is laid up for me a **crown of righteousness,** which the Lord, the righteous judge, shall give me at that day: and not to me only, but unto all them also that love his appearing.

Paul faced death often and suffered much at the hands of the Jews and the Gentiles. He never sorrowed for having followed Jesus but was looking forward to seeing him in heaven after his death. Paul kept his eyes on the prize of the high calling and finished his course. What a beautiful day that must have been. He had fought the good fight; he had kept the faith. He had been made righteous with Christ righteousness and now wears a crown of righteousness. Set before everyone on this earth are life and death. Life is a choice we must make every day. At the end of our earthly quest for the abundant life in Christ, we shall find the ultimate blessings of God's Kingdom and worship face to face LIFE HIMSELF! Praise JESUS! Any crowns we receive we shall throw at his feet in adoration and worship.

LESSON 11

Gift of Faith

OBJECTIVE: Develop and demonstrate an understanding of the working of faith.

GIFT OF FAITH

Rom 10:17 So then **faith cometh by hearing**, and hearing by the word of God.

Every man begins with the measure of faith given by God. Faith comes by hearing God's word, and his word brings understanding. As we plant the word of faith in our hearts, it multiplies to a more significant measure. All that we do in God's kingdom is by faith. In the parable of the sower, Jesus said that everyone who has an understanding of the word of the kingdom of God would obtain more. The one who does not understand, even what he thinks he has will be taken away. God's word planted in good soil brings forth fruit which yields a greater abundance of seeds for the sower.

> **Eph 2:8**   For by grace are ye saved **through faith**; and that not of yourselves: it is **the gift of God:**
>
> **Gal 2:20**   I am crucified with Christ: nevertheless I live; yet not I, but Christ liveth in me: and the life which I now live in the flesh I live by **the faith of the Son of God,** who loved me, and gave himself for me.
>
> **Rom 12:3**   For I say, through the grace given unto me, to every man that is among you, not to think *of himself* more highly than he ought to think; bu to think soberly, according as **God hath dealt to every man the measure of faith.**

In Galatians, Paul points out that we cannot work the miracles of God except by the hearing of faith. It is crucial that we hear God first, then the faith will be present to perform the work. In (Rom. 12:6) it says that he that prophesies should prophesy according to the proportion of faith. The word proportion means the intensity of something said. We can only communicate by faith and minister according to the intensity of how we hear the Spirit say it. The more sensitive to the Spirit's voice, the deeper our faith walk in the Spirit, and the more we will be useful ministering the Spirit to others. It is important to the body as a whole for each of us to operate in our different gifts of grace.

> **Gal 3:5**   He therefore that ministereth to you the Spirit, and worketh miracles among you, *doeth he it* by the works of the law, or by the **hearing of faith?**
>
> **Heb 11:1**   Now **faith** is the substance of things hoped for, the **evidence** of things not seen.

Faith is a gift from God that we might believe and be saved. Faith is a spiritual substance and a spiritual evidence that bears witness and revives and energizes the spirit of man thus ultimately affecting this earthly realm.

FAITH AS A GRAIN OF MUSTARD SEED

Luk 17:1   Then said he unto the disciples, It is impossible but that offences will come: but woe *unto him,* through whom they come!

Luk 17:2   It were better for him that a millstone were hanged about his neck, and he cast into the sea, than that he should offend one of these little ones.

Luk 17:3   Take heed to yourselves: If thy brother trespass against thee, rebuke him; and if he repent, forgive him.

Luk 17:4   And if he trespass against thee seven times in a day, and seven times in a day turn again to thee, saying, I repent; **thou shalt forgive him.**

Luk 17:5   And the apostles said unto the Lord, Increase our faith.

Luk 17:6   And the Lord said, If ye had **faith as a grain of mustard seed,** ye might say unto this sycamine tree, Be thou plucked up by the root, and be thou planted in the sea; and it should obey you.

Luk 17:7   But which of you, having **a servant** plowing or feeding cattle, will say unto him by and by, when he is come from the field, Go and sit down to meat?

Luk 17:8   And will not rather say unto him, Make ready wherewith I may sup, and gird thyself, and **serve**

me, till I have eaten and drunken; and afterward thou shalt eat and drink?

Luk 17:9 Doth he thank that servant because he did the things that were commanded him? I trow not.

Luk 17:10 So likewise ye, when ye shall have done all those things which are commanded you, say, We are unprofitable servants: we have done that which was **our duty** to do.

Jesus was teaching the disciples about love and forgiveness, and they wanted their faith increased. His response was to tell them a story about being a servant and says to do likewise. What was it about the servant that we are supposed to do also? What is the significance of this story? The servant was supposed to obey the word of the master to serve the master above his wants or needs. To love God first is the first commandment (duty) we have. The second commandment is to love others. If we offend a little one, it would be better for us if a millstone were tied around our neck and cast into the sea. Love forgives over and over, and when we are offended, we are to forgive and say it is my duty. Jesus did answer their question about how to increase their faith. Faith obeys God's word and works by love and without doing our duty to love, our faith would not be active. Unless we are under the authority of God (obedient), no sycamine tree or mountain will move in response to our command.

Mat 13:31 Another parable put he forth unto them, saying, The kingdom of heaven is like to a **grain of mustard seed,** which a man took, and sowed in his field:

Mat 13:32 Which indeed is the **least of all seeds**: but **when it is grown,** it is the **greatest among herbs**, and becometh a tree, so that the birds of the air come and lodge in the branches thereof.

What kind of faith does a grain of mustard seed have? The parable of the kingdom of heaven shows the mustard seed which is least in size of all herb seeds grows and becomes the greatest of herbs. That is what the faith of the Son of God does. God's kind of faith grows in us and through us becomes a refuge for others.

Faith that can remove mountains takes time to grow from that seed to the full fruit in the tree unless the Holy Spirit supernaturally imparts it as a working of miracles. It is not the size of our faith, but the quality (kind) of faith: living or dead, little or great.

LITTLE FAITH VS GREAT FAITH

In (Mat 6) Jesus said to seek first the kingdom of God and his righteousness, and all the things we need in life will be provided. If we are not trusting God for the basic needs in life, we have little faith. If we are fearful, we have little faith. If we have little understanding of God's Word, we have little faith. When we seek God first, he gives us understanding, faith, and the benefits of his Kingdom.

Mat 6:30   Wherefore, if God so clothe the grass of the field, which to day is, and to morrow is cast into the oven, *shall he* not much more *clothe* you, **O ye of little faith?**

Mat 6:31   Therefore take no thought, saying, What shall we eat? or, What shall we drink? or, Wherewithal shall we be clothed?

Mat 8:26   And he saith unto them, Why are ye fearful, **O ye of little faith?** Then he arose, and rebuked the winds and the sea; and there was a great calm.

Mat 8:27   But the men marvelled, saying, What manner of man is this, that even the winds and the sea obey him!

Mat 16:6   Then Jesus said unto them, Take heed and beware of the **leaven** of the Pharisees and of the Sadducees.

Mat 16:7   And they reasoned among themselves, saying, *It is* because we have taken no bread.

Mat 16:8   *Which* when Jesus perceived, he said unto them, **O ye of little faith,** why reason ye among yourselves, because ye have brought no bread?

The disciples did not understand what Jesus meant when he was teaching about the leaven of the Pharisees because of their carnal reasoning. Jesus told them they had little faith because they did not consider the miracle of the loaves and fishes. God is more than able to provide bread.

Jesus was teaching the disciples to beware of the leaven (teaching) of the Pharisees. How did that relate to them forgetting to bring food?

We can't point fingers because most likely we have done the same at some point in our walk with Christ. If we neglect to worship, think upon his word and be grateful for what God has done for us, it will be, O we of little faith.

Mat 8:5   And when Jesus was entered into Capernaum, there came unto him a centurion, beseeching him.

Mat 8:6   And saying, Lord, my servant lieth at home sick of the palsy, grievously tormented.

Mat 8:7   And Jesus saith unto him, I will come and heal him.

Mat 8:8   The centurion answered and said, Lord, I am not worthy that thou shouldest come under my roof: but **speak the word only,** and my servant shall be healed.

Mat 8:9 For I am a man under authority, having soldiers under me: and I say to this *man,* Go, and he goeth; and to another, Come, and he cometh; and to my servant, Do this, and he doeth *it.*

Mat 8:10 When Jesus heard *it,* he marvelled, and said to them that followed, Verily I say unto you, I have not found **so great faith,** no, not in Israel.

What was it that made this man's faith so great that Jesus would marvel? This man understood the authority and power that Jesus operated in was a much higher authority than this Centurions commission under Rome. Great faith recognizes that Jesus authority is from above and is above all other and his kingdom greater than any of this earth. The Centurion's words carried the weight of Rome. Jesus words carried the weight of the kingdom of God. The woman whose daughter was vexed by a devil exhibited great faith. She humbled herself and worshipped, and though being called a dog, she reasoned that even the dogs received mercy and were allowed to eat the food that fell from the master's table. The Jews considered Gentiles as dogs, yet she believed the Messiah would accept even one considered a dog. What great faith she showed in God's promise of mercy to all nations. Even the Gentiles had hope in the Messiah's coming (Isa 11:10; 42:1,6).

Mat 15:25 Then came she and worshipped him, saying, Lord, help me.

Mat 15:26 But he answered and said, It is not meet to take the children's bread, and to cast *it* to dogs.

Mat 15:27 And she said, Truth, Lord: yet the dogs eat of the crumbs which fall from their masters' table.

Mat 15:28   Then Jesus answered and said unto her, O woman, **great *is* thy faith:** be it unto thee even as thou wilt. And her daughter was made whole from that very hour.

TAKE HEED HOW YOU HEAR

Mat 13:9   Who hath ears to hear, let him hear.

Mat 13:10   And the disciples came, and said unto him, Why speakest thou unto them in parables?

Mat 13:11   He answered and said unto them, Because it is given unto you to know the mysteries of the kingdom of heaven, but to them it is not given.

Mat 13:12   For whosoever hath, to him shall be given, and **he shall have more abundance:** but whosoever hath not, from him shall be taken away even that he hath.

Luk 8:18   **Take heed therefore how ye hear**: for whosoever hath, to him shall be given; and whosoever hath not, from him shall be taken **even that which he seemeth to have.**

The knowledge of the mysteries of the Kingdom of Heaven is given only to the disciples of Christ; those who believed the word regarding the kingdom of God and God's Son, Jesus (Mat 13:1-12). The disciples had faith in Christ; their hearts were good ground. Jesus said they who have, are given more abundance. Those who do not have faith, what they have (or seem to have) shall be taken away. Why? Because it was not rooted and grounded in Christ Jesus who is the Beginning and the End and who is the foundation stone of our faith (1Pe 2:5-8). Those who listen attentively and obey are given more revelation resulting in more abundance of faith in God. That is why Jesus said to take heed how you hear. Be doers of the word and not hearers only, deceiving your selves (Jas 1:22). Judas was a thief who pilfered from the common treasury of the band of disciples. He was deluding himself, his greed choking out the truth Jesus taught and the witness of the miracles that followed.

FAITH IN HIS NAME

> Luk 19:38 Saying, Blessed *be* the King that **cometh in the name of the Lord:** peace in heaven, and glory in the highest.

Jesus came to earth with the authority and power of his Father's name, and he manifested his Father's name (Joh 17). The name of God is sacred. His name reflects his glory. God's names are affiliated with his acts: for example, he is Jehovah Rapha, the God who heals (Exo 15:26). We see that name manifested in Christ who went about doing good and healing all that were oppressed of the devil. God also was revealed by other such names, i.e., Jehovah our righteousness, Jehovah our peace, Jehovah, our provider. Jesus is made unto us wisdom, righteousness, sanctification, and redemption (ransom for our peace). His name is above every name. In his name Jesus, Jehovah our salvation is manifested, and the righteousness of God is revealed.

> Joh 17:6 I have manifested thy name unto the men which thou gavest me out of the world: thine they were, and thou gavest them Me; and they have kept thy word.

> Php 2:9 Wherefore God also hath highly exalted him, and given him a **name which is above every name:**

Php 2:10 That **at the name of Jesus** every knee should bow, of *things* in heaven, and *things* in earth, and *things* under the earth;

Php 2:11 And *that* every tongue should confess that **Jesus Christ** *is* **Lord,** to the glory of God the Father.

Mar 16:17 And these signs shall follow **them that believe**; **In my name** shall they cast out devils; they shall speak with new tongues;

Mar 16:18 They shall take up serpents; and if they drink any deadly thing, it shall not hurt them; they shall lay hands on the sick, and they shall recover.

When we call on the name of Jesus we are calling on the authority and the power of his kingdom. His name is exalted high above every name, and signs follow those whose faith is by him.

Act 3:16 And **his name through faith in his name hath made this man strong,** whom ye see and know: yea, the faith which is by him hath given him this perfect soundness in the presence of you all.

Gal 2:20 I am crucified with Christ: nevertheless I live; yet not I, but Christ liveth in me: and the life which I now live in the flesh I live **by the faith of the Son of God,** who loved me, and gave himself for me.

AMBASSADORS

We are his ambassadors sent in Jesus name into the world to preach the gospel and make known his righteousness.

2Co 5:17 Therefore if any man *be* in Christ, *he is* a new creature: old things are passed away; behold, all things are become new.

2Co 5:18 And all things *are* of God, who hath reconciled us to himself by Jesus Christ, and **hath given to us the ministry of reconciliation;**

2Co 5:19 To wit, that **God was in Christ, reconciling the world** unto himself, **not imputing their trespasses** unto them; and hath committed unto us the word of reconciliation.

2Co 5:20 Now then **we are ambassadors for Christ**, as though God did beseech *you* by us: we pray *you* in Christ's stead, be ye reconciled to God.

2Co 5:21 For he hath made him *to be* sin for us, who knew no sin; that we might be made the righteousness of God in him.

- ambassador—act as a representative (fig. preacher).
- reconciliation—exchange, restoration to divine favor, atonement.
- imputing—take inventory or account.

An ambassador seeks peace and as such our feet are shod with the gospel of peace. Our ministry is a ministry of reconciliation to let the world know that God is not holding their sins against them and is offering peace through his Son. God wants to restore to divine favor those who believe in Jesus, who was the atonement.

LESSON 12

Gifts of God

OBJECTIVE: Develop and demonstrate an understanding of the gifts of God.

7 GRACE GIFTS

Rom 12:3   For I say, through the grace given unto me, to every man that is among you, not to think *of himself* more highly than he ought to think; but to think soberly, according as God hath dealt to every man the measure of faith.

Rom 12:4   For as we have many members in one body, and all members have not the same **office:**

Rom 12:5   So we, *being* many, are one body in Christ, and every one members one of another.

- gifts—divine gratuity, spiritual endowment.
- office—practice, act, function.

We are one body and members of one another. Each member functions to contribute to the wholeness of the body. All members of the body will find their job descriptions, so to speak, in the gifts of grace listed in verses 6-8. We each have various gifts that work together for the benefit of the whole body of Christ. We will not all function the same way but accordingly as God has gifted us individually. God's grace has blessed each with the equal measure of faith and only by his grace will our part in his work yield an increase. Therefore let us understand and confess our total dependence upon him in all that we undertake in his name.

1. PROPHECY/PROPHESY

Rom 12:6 Having then **gifts differing according to the grace that is given to us,** whether prophecy, *let us prophesy* according to the **proportion of faith;**

Rom 12:7 Or ministry, *let us wait* on *our* ministering: or he that teacheth, on teaching;

Rom 12:8 Or he that exhorteth, on exhortation: he that giveth, *let him do it* with simplicity; he that ruleth, with diligence; he that sheweth mercy, with cheerfulness.

The phrase let us prophesy according to the proportion of faith is hearing and speaking the message with the intensity of the Spirit (Rom 12:6). One can prophesy by teaching or preaching or by the gift of prophecy with a specific word in a particular time (1Co 12). We must allow the Holy Spirit to be in charge and not quench him.

- prophecy/prophesy—prediction/speak by inspiration.

Act 2:16 But this is that which was spoken by the prophet Joel;

Act 2:17 And it shall come to pass in the last days, saith God, I will pour out of my Spirit upon all flesh: and your sons and your daughters shall **prophesy,** and your young men shall see **visions,** and your old men shall **dream dreams:**

Act 2:18 And on my servants and on my handmaidens I will pour out in those days of my Spirit; and **they shall prophesy:**

- (Acts 21:8-14) Philip's 3 daughters/prophetesses & The Prophet Agabus

1Co14:3 But he that **prophesieth** speaketh unto men to edification, and exhortation, and comfort.

- edification—building up.
- exhortation—call near, comfort.

Prophesying is speaking under the inspiration of the Holy Spirit. Those in (Act 2) were speaking in tongues, and it was called prophesying. They were speaking forth the wonderful works of God. Visions and dreams are prophetic also.

One can prophesy and not be a prophet, yet a prophet will prophesy whether by prediction or by expounding the word of God.

2. MINISTRY

- ministry—servant, teacher, deacon.

After the disciples prayed they laid hands on Stephen and other men and set them apart for service of the daily administration to the needs of the saints (Act 6). Note that they wanted men full of wisdom and the Holy Spirit. The ministry of Deacon is a helps ministry to those whose primary ministry is in the Word and Prayer. God used Stephen in the service of a deacon, and he had great wisdom and ministered in the gift of miracles.

- (Acts 6:1-8) Stephen—helped serve in the daily administration—serve tables—did great miracles)

- (Rom 16:1,2) Phoebe—assistant of many (Col 4:12)

- (Phm 1:23) Epaphras—labored fervently in prayer, fellow prisoner with Paul

- (Ro 16:3-5; Ro 18:24-26) Priscilla and Aquila—Paul's helpers, teachers, possibly pastors

1Ti 3:12   And let these also **first be proved**; then let them use the office of a deacon, being found blameless.

1Ti 3:13   For they that have used **the office of a deacon** well purchase to themselves a good degree, and great boldness in the faith which is in Christ Jesus.

- good degree—grade of dignity.

Php 1:1   Paul and Timotheus, the servants of Jesus Christ, to all the saints in Christ Jesus which are at Philippi, with the **bishops and deacons**:

Some are called into the ministry of preaching and teaching God's Word, others to minister alongside. Their gifts function in various forms through the talents given each. Paul counted himself a servant and was thankful that God counted him faithful, putting him into the ministry. All who have answered the call are servants of God. Jesus said those of us that want to be the greatest should be the servant of all. We are all called to serve God together in a church body, each adding to the edification and growth as he functions in his gift.

> **Mat 20:26** But it shall not be so among you: but whosoever will be great among you, let him be your **minister;**

> **Mat 20:27** And whosoever will be chief among you, let him be your **servant:**

> **Mat 20:28** Even as **the Son of man** came not to be ministered unto, but to minister, and to give his life a ransom for many.

> **1Ti 1:12** And I thank Christ Jesus our Lord, who hath enabled me, for that he counted me faithful, **putting me into the ministry;**

3. TEACHING

- teaching—instruction.
- (Col 1:28) The Apostle Paul.
- (Matt 28:20) Jesus and the Disciples.
- (Act 18:26) Priscilla and Aquila.

Priscilla and Aquila accompanied Paul on some of his journeys. Paul preached, but he also taught, and so did those he took with him to train and help him in the ministry.

> **Col 1:28** Whom we preach, warning every man, and **teaching** every man in all wisdom; **that we may present every man perfect** in Christ Jesus:

Col 1:29 Whereunto I also labour, striving **according to his working**, which worketh in me mightily.

Col 3:16 Let the word of Christ dwell in you richly in all wisdom; **teaching and admonishing one another** in psalms and hymns and spiritual songs, singing with grace in your hearts to the Lord.

Col 3:17 And whatsoever ye do in word or deed, **do all in the name of the Lord Jesus**, giving thanks to God and the Father by him.

God had Moses teach the children of Israel a song so they would remember the word of the Lord. At the end of the days, they will be reminded and see the condition of their heart and repent from their sins (Deu 31:30—32:1-43). Music carries the message in a form that helps the heart to remember.

4. EXHORTATION

- exhortation—call near, implore, solace, comfort, entreaty.
- (Lk 3:15-18) The prophet John the Baptist.
- (2 Co 5:19-21) The Apostle Paul.

Act 11:22 Then tidings of these things came unto the ears of the church which was in Jerusalem: and they sent forth Barnabas, that he should go as far as Antioch.

Act 11:23 Who, when he came, and had seen the grace of God, was glad, and **exhorted them** all, that with purpose of heart they would cleave unto the Lord.

Heb 3:13   But **exhort one another daily,** while it is called To day; lest any of you be hardened through the deceitfulness of sin.

Heb 3:14   For we are made partakers of Christ, if we hold the beginning of our confidence stedfast unto the end;

1Th 4:1   Furthermore then we beseech you, brethren, and **exhort** you by the Lord Jesus, that as ye have received of us how ye ought to walk and to please God, so ye would abound more and more.

Heb 13:22   And I beseech you, brethren, suffer the **word of exhortation**: for I have written a letter unto you in few words.

Exhortations call us near to God and challenge us to walk according to the Spirit. It reminds us to hold fast and look to the future at the reward of following Jesus. One with a gift of exhortation sees potential in every person and is moved by the Spirit to comfort them and to challenge them to do their best. They may even give solutions or steps for accomplishing this transformation.

5. GIVING

Rom 12:10   Be kindly affectioned one to another with brotherly love; in honour preferring one another;

Rom 12:11   Not slothful in business; fervent in spirit; serving the Lord;

Rom 12:12   Rejoicing in hope; patient in tribulation; continuing instant in prayer;

Rom 12:13 Distributing to the necessity of saints; given to hospitality.

- (Matt 27:57-61) Joseph of Arimathea
- (Lk 8:3) Joanna, Susanna & others
- (Acts 16:14-15) Lydia
- (Acts 9:36) Dorcas

This instruction is for all the saints to affectionate toward one another and give honor to each other. We are admonished to be fervent in spirit in our service to our God. It is his will that those who are able assist in helping the saints in need.

- hospitality—to entertain strangers.

1Pe 4:9 Use hospitality one to another without grudging.

1Ti 6:17 Charge them that are rich in this world, that they be not highminded, nor trust in uncertain riches, but in the living God, who giveth us richly all things to enjoy;

1Ti 6:18 That they do good, that they be rich in good works, **ready to distribute, willing to communicate;**

1Ti 6:19 Laying up in store for themselves a good foundation against the time to come, that they may lay hold on eternal life.

During Jesus ministry, he was followed by many who ministered to him out of their substance (Lk 8:3). One such disciple was Joanna wife of Chuza, Herod's steward. Those believers with riches are instructed not to trust in those riches but to be rich in good works, ready to distribute to help others. Instead of storing up riches on earth, lay up treasures in heaven.

Hospitality is not only for the rich to consider but for all who name the name of Jesus. In the culture of that day hospitality to strangers was common. Neither is giving merely for the rich. The widow who put in 2 mites in the treasury put in more than all the rich men because she gave out of her need, they out of their treasures. The gift of giving can take on many forms.

> **Act 9:36** Now there was at Joppa a certain disciple named Tabitha, which by interpretation is called Dorcas: this woman was full of good works and almsdeeds which she did.

Dorcas was dearly loved for her kindness and generosity. She made garments and coats for the widows and when she died they sent for Peter to raise her up (Act 9:39).

6. RULING

- (1 Tim 5:17) elders
- (Acts 14:23) (elders)

> **Act 14:23** And when they had **ordained them elders** in every church, and had prayed with fasting, they commended them to the Lord, on whom they believed.

> **1Ti 3:1** This is a true saying, If a man desire the **office of a bishop**, he desireth a good work.

- bishop—superintendent.

The Apostle Paul established churches and ordained elders to rule over the flock of God; to guide and teach and train up men to teach and minister. The Bishop and Pastor are the same office.

7. MERCY

- mercy—have compassion, pity on.
- (Lk 10:30-37) The Samaritan.
- (Acts 9:36) Tabitha/Dorcas.

Those who have compassion and feed the poor and minister to the sick have a gift of mercy. The Samaritan showed mercy to a man who was robbed and beaten. He cleansed his wounds and also paid the expenses for his continued care. Dorcas gift of mercy led her to do many good works and to give to the poor. She used the talents God gave her and made coats and garments for the widows. Nurses are often called angels of mercy because they care for those who cannot care for themselves. Their whole life is a life of showing compassion to others, of being a servant. Some feel called to feed the poor or help the homeless or help provide for their needs. There are other opportunities to show mercy, and if that is your gift, they will find you.

5 GIFTS TO PERFECT

Eph 4:7 But **unto every one of us is given grace** according to the **measure of the gift of Christ.**

Eph 4:8 Wherefore he saith, When he ascended up on high, he led captivity captive, and **gave gifts unto men.**

Eph 4:9 (Now that he ascended, what is it but that he also descended first into the lower parts of the earth?

Eph 4:10 He that descended is the same also that ascended up far above all heavens, that he might fill all things.

Eph 4:11 And **he gave** some, apostles; and some, prophets; and some, evangelists; and some, pastors and teachers;

Eph 4:12 For the **perfecting** of the saints, for the **work** of the ministry, for the **edifying** of the body of Christ:

Eph 4:13 Till we all come in the unity of the faith, and of the knowledge of the Son of God, unto a perfect man, unto the measure of the stature of the fulness of Christ:

The perfecting of the saints means the complete furnishing in this verse. The saints are to be furnished, equipped in the word and in character for the work they are called to do.

1. Apostles—delegate, ambassador of the gospel, sent one—elder.
2. Prophets—a foreteller or/and inspired speaker (Acts 21:10) Agabas.
3. Evangelists—preacher of the gospel (Acts 21:8) Philip.
4. Pastors—shepherds–(1 Pet 5:1-4) elders (1 Tim) Timothy.
5. Teachers—an instructor.

These five gifts are messengers that handle the Word of God to train and perfect the saints that they also may do the work of the ministry that the Church may be edified. These gifts are given to the Church until we come into the unity of faith, knowledge of Jesus, and the perfect image of Christ. That means the ministry of Apostle and Prophet have not passed away as many would like to believe, but will continue until Christ returns. At that point, we are wholly made perfect into Christ image, spirit, soul and body. Until then we are to occupy until Christ comes and train God's people to do the work of the ministry.

Paul told Timothy whom he had appointed elder of the church in Ephesus that God's word is profitable for doctrine, reproof, correction and instruction that the man of God may be perfect, thoroughly furnished for every good work. Jesus said the works he did we would also do, and even greater works (Joh 14). All men and women of God should aspire to be perfected and become thoroughly furnished to do those works God has ordained for him/her in Christ.

> **2Ti 3:16** All scripture is given by inspiration of God, and is profitable for doctrine, for reproof, for correction, for instruction in righteousness:
>
> **2Ti 3:17** That the man of God may be **perfect**, throughly furnished unto all good works.
>
> **Col 1:28** Whom we preach, warning every man, and **teaching** every man in all wisdom; **that we may present every man perfect** in Christ Jesus:
>
> **Col 1:29** Whereunto I also labour, striving according to his working, which worketh in me mightily.

QUALIFICATIONS FOR AN ELDER

The elder is called and equipped to function in the gift of ruling. It is through this office that his other gifts find their expression. Elders should know sound doctrine and be able to exhort others, be willing to take oversight with a ready mind and be examples to the flock.

> **Tit 1:4** To Titus, mine own son after the common faith: Grace, mercy, and peace, from God the Father and the Lord Jesus Christ our Saviour.

Tit 1:5 For this cause left I thee in Crete, that thou shouldest set in order the things that are wanting, and **ordain elders in every city,** as I had appointed thee:

Tit 1:6 If any be blameless, the husband of one wife, having faithful children not accused of riot or unruly.

Tit 1:7 For **a bishop must be blameless, as the steward of God;** not selfwilled, not soon angry, not given to wine, no striker, not given to filthy lucre;

Tit 1:8 But a lover of hospitality, a lover of good men, sober, just, holy, temperate;

Tit 1:9 **Holding fast the faithful word as he hath been taught,** that he may be able by **sound doctrine both to exhort and to convince** the gainsayers.

The only way to accomplish the perfecting of the saints in the unity of the faith and knowledge of Jesus is by the preaching and teaching of God's word by those given as gifts to men. God calls into the work of the ministry those He has found faithful, those He has proven.

God has given spiritual, moral, and maturity guidelines for those to be considered elders of the church. Elders are under-shepherds to the chief Shepherd who shall reward us according to our faithfulness. The shepherd does not beat the sheep into compliance with God's word but is an example of faith, love, and mercy.

1Pe 5:1 **The elders** which are among you I exhort, who am also an elder, and a witness of the sufferings of Christ, and also a partaker of the glory that shall be revealed:

1Pe 5:2 **Feed the flock of God** which is among you, **taking the oversight** thereof, not by constraint, but willingly; not for filthy lucre, but of a ready mind;

1Pe 5:3 Neither as being lords over God's heritage, but being ensamples to the flock.

1Pe 5:4 And when the **chief Shepherd** shall appear, ye shall receive a crown of glory that fadeth not away.

SPIRITUAL GIFTS

1Co 12:1 Now **concerning spiritual gifts,** brethren, I would not have you ignorant.

- ignorant—lack of knowledge

1Co 12:2 Ye know that ye were Gentiles, carried away unto these dumb idols, even as ye were led.

1Co 12:3 Wherefore I give you to understand, that no man speaking by the Spirit of God calleth Jesus accursed: and that no man can say that **Jesus is the Lord, but by the Holy Ghost.**

Our Heavenly Father does not want us to lack knowledge of what he has given to the Church through his Son. God is not a dumb idol who cannot see or hear or speak nor move. He is The Living God, the Almighty One. He has chosen to use the body of Christ to minister to the body of Christ through various endowments of the Holy Spirit. Our Father still speaks and moves today through these gifts. He would not give us anything that would not honor or glorify his holy son. Any spirit that would curse Jesus is not God's

Holy Spirit. By the Holy Spirit we are enlightened to the truth and confess that Jesus Christ is Lord, and we are baptized into the body of Christ Jesus by him.

Rom 10:9   That if thou shalt **confess with thy mouth the Lord Jesus,** and shalt believe in thine heart that God hath raised him from the dead, thou shalt be saved.

THE TRINITY WORKING TOGETHER

1Co 12:4   Now there are diversities of gifts, but the same Spirit.

1Co 12:5   And there are differences of administrations, but the same Lord.

1Co 12:6   And there are diversities of operations, but it is the same God which worketh all in all.

There are diversities of spiritual endowments (gifts) but the same Holy Spirit dividing the gifts to us as He wills. There are differences of administrations or services/ministries but the same Lord who is head over all the church government. There are diversities of operations/workings, but it is the same God (Father) which works all these gifts in us. Jesus said it was the Father in him that does the works. The Father, Son, and Holy Spirit dwell within us who believe in the Son (Joh 14).

1Co 12:7   But **the manifestation of the Spirit is given to every man to profit withal.**

1Co 12:8   For to one is given by the Spirit the word of wisdom; to another the word of knowledge by the same Spirit;

1Co 12:9 To another faith by the same Spirit; to another the gifts of healing by the same Spirit;

1Co 12:10 To another the working of miracles; to another prophecy; to another discerning of spirits; to another *divers* kinds of tongues; to another the interpretation of tongues:

1Co 12:11 But all these worketh that one and the selfsame Spirit, dividing to every man severally as he will.

9 MANIFESTATIONS OF THE SPIRIT

The manifestation of the Spirit is given to profit all in the body and bring glory to God. Each one is given Spiritual gifts as the Holy Spirit's wisdom divides them to us. As we yield to the Spirit's working through us with the unique gifts he has allotted, we are being built up together as a spiritual habitation of God. The more we help others, the more we grow spiritually and experience transformation. God has set each one in the body as it pleased him. One member of the body cannot say to the other I have no need of you for every member is vital to the body's function (1 Co 12:18-21). God has especially gifted us each that we might fit together fulfilling the needs of the Church. As we yield to the Holy Spirit, we will begin to flow in those gifts under the supernatural power of God.

1. WORD OF WISDOM

- word—something said, discourse on a topic.

The Word of Wisdom is a word imparted through a believer in speaking for the benefit of the body of Christ. It could be wisdom needed regarding a specific matter concerning the church or an individual. It could be regarding an issue in the present or the future. After Jesus healed the man, who had paralysis at the pool of Bethesda he cautioned him with a word of wisdom. The word of wisdom was that if he continued in sin, it would result in something worse coming on him (Jon 5:1-14). It could be that his sin opened the door for the condition from which Jesus healed him at the pool.

> Joh 5:14 Afterward Jesus findeth him in the temple, and said unto him, Behold, thou art made whole: sin no more, lest a worse thing come unto thee.

2. WORD OF KNOWLEDGE

The Word of Knowledge is a word imparted to a believer showing God's knowledge of a situation. In (Joh 1), Jesus, while speaking to the woman at the well revealed that she had married five times and the man she now lived with was not her husband. That was a Word of Knowledge that convinced the woman that he was a prophet and caused her to believe he was Messiah and she immediately went to testify to the town (Joh 1:1-42).

3. FAITH

This gift of faith is not the same as the faith in Romans chapter 12 of which every man has a measure. This gift of faith is a supernatural move of the Holy Spirit within a person at that moment to believe for the impossible.

> Act 14:8 And there sat a certain man at Lystra, impotent in his feet, being a cripple from his mother's womb, who never had walked:

> Act 14:9 The same heard Paul speak: who stedfastly beholding him, and **perceiving that he had faith to be healed.**

Act 14:10   Said with a loud voice, Stand upright on thy feet. And he leaped and walked.

4. GIFTS OF HEALING

Mat 4:23   And Jesus went about all Galilee, teaching in their synagogues, and preaching the gospel of the kingdom, and **healing all manner of sickness and all manner of disease** among the people.

Mat 4:24   And his fame went throughout all Syria: and they brought unto him all sick people that were taken with divers diseases and torments, and those which were possessed with devils, and those which were lunatick, and those that had the palsy; and he healed them.

Act 5:16   There came also a multitude *out* of the cities round about unto Jerusalem, bringing sick folks, and them which were vexed with unclean spirits: and they were **healed** every one.

5. WORKING OF MIRACLES

Act 19:11   And **God wrought special miracles** by the hands of Paul:

Act 19:12   So that from his body were brought unto the sick handkerchiefs or aprons, and the diseases departed from them, and the evil spirits went out of them.

Act 5:15 Insomuch that they brought forth the sick into the streets, and laid *them* on beds and couches, that at the least **the shadow of Peter** passing by might overshadow some of them.

He that works miracles among us does it by the hearing of faith (Gal 3:5).

6. PROPHECY

The gift of prophecy is manifested as either a prediction or a word of exhortation supernaturally by the Spirit. In (Act 21), Agabus the prophet predicted that Paul would be bound by the Romans when he went to Jerusalem. It was not to deter Paul from going to Jerusalem but a confirmation to him of God's plan. Paul's captivity would be an occasion for him to give testimony before Roman officials and kings and preach the gospel of Christ. Many times a prophecy will be a confirmation to something God has already communicated.

Act 21:10 And as we tarried *there* many days, there came down from Judaea a certain prophet, named Agabus.

Act 21:11 And when he was come unto us, he took Paul's girdle, and bound his own hands and feet, and said, **Thus saith the Holy Ghost,** So shall the Jews at Jerusalem bind the man that owneth this girdle, and shall deliver *him* into the hands of the Gentiles.

Act 21:12 And when we heard these things, both we, and they of that place, besought him not to go up to Jerusalem.

Act 21:13 Then Paul answered, What mean ye to weep and to break mine heart? for I am ready not to be bound only, but also to die at Jerusalem for the name of the Lord Jesus.

Act 21:14 And when he would not be persuaded, we ceased, saying, The will of the Lord be done.

7. DISCERNING OF SPIRITS

Act 16:16 And it came to pass, as we went to prayer, a certain damsel possessed with **a spirit of divination** met us, which brought her masters much gain by soothsaying:

Act 16:17 The same followed Paul and us, and cried, saying, These men are the servants of the most high God, which shew unto us the way of salvation.

Act 16:18 And this did she many days. But Paul, being grieved, turned and said to the spirit, I command thee in the name of Jesus Christ to come out of her. And he came out the same hour.

Act 8:22 Repent therefore of this thy wickedness, and pray God, if perhaps the thought of thine heart may be forgiven thee.

Act 8:23 For **I perceive** that thou art in the gall of bitterness, and *in* the bond of iniquity.

Jesus operated in this gift all the time, and he cast out many devils. The gift of discernment is not only for discerning evil spirits or an evil attitude but angels and good attitudes. In the following scripture, Jesus discerns a spirit of integrity in Nathanael, even having a vision of him sitting under the fig tree.

Joh 1:47   Jesus saw Nathanael coming to him, and saith of him, Behold an Israelite indeed, **in whom is no guile!**

Joh 1:48   Nathanael saith unto him, Whence knowest thou me? Jesus answered and said unto him, Before that Philip called thee, when thou wast under the fig tree, **I saw thee.**

Mat 8:16   When the even was come, they brought unto him many that were possessed with devils: and **he cast out the spirits with *his* word,** and healed all that were sick:

Act 8:26   And the **angel of the Lord** spake unto Philip, saying, Arise, and go toward the south unto the way that goeth down from Jerusalem unto Gaza, which is desert.

The angel of the Lord gave instructions to Philip in this scenario. Philip would need discernment of spirits because Satan and his cohorts, both spiritual and physical can appear as messengers of light (2Co 11:14-15).

8.   DIVERS KINDS OF TONGUES

This is referring to the diverse languages of men as seen in (Act 2)when the Holy Spirit was poured out and they began to speak in tongues.

Act 2:2   And suddenly there came a sound from heaven as of a rushing mighty wind, and it filled all the house where they were sitting.

Act 2:3   And there appeared unto them **cloven tongues** like as of fire, and it sat upon each of them.

Act 2:4 And they were all filled with the Holy Ghost, and began to speak with other tongues, as the Spirit gave them utterance.

Act 2:5 And there were dwelling at Jerusalem Jews, devout men, out of every nation under heaven.

Act 2:6 Now when this was noised abroad, the multitude came together, and were confounded, because that every man heard them speak in his own language.

People were gathered there from out of every nation. The text says they heard them speaking the wonderful works of God in their native languages. The people knew that those speaking were Galileans and wondered how they knew their languages. God used tongues to help convince those from other nations to believe. Tongues are a sign for the unbeliever according to Paul in (1Co 14).

9. INTERPRETATION OF TONGUES

Messages in tongues in the congregation should be interpreted that the body of Christ may be exhorted and edified. In Acts 2 the people heard them speak in his language. They could understand the messages given. In the congregation, if there is no interpretation one should keep silent and talk to himself and God.

1Co 14:16 How is it then, brethren? when ye come together, every one of you hath a psalm, hath a doctrine, hath a tongue, hath a revelation, hath an interpretation. **Let all things be done unto edifying**.

1Co 14:27 If any man speak in an *unknown* tongue, *let it be* by two, or at the most *by* three, and *that* by course; and let one interpret.

1Co 14:28 But **if there be no interpreter, let him keep silence** in the church; and **let him speak to himself, and to God.**

STEWARDSHIP

MINISTER YOUR GIFT TO ONE ANOTHER

1Pe 4:8 And above all things have fervent charity among yourselves: for charity shall cover the multitude of sins.

1Pe 4:9 Use hospitality one to another without grudging.

1Pe 4:10 **As every man hath received the gift, even so minister the same one to another, as good stewards of the manifold grace of God.**

1Pe 4:11 If any man speak, let him speak as the oracles of God; if any man minister, let him do it as of the ability which God giveth: that God in all things may be glorified through Jesus Christ, to whom be praise and dominion for ever and ever. Amen.

- steward—manager, overseer.

As stewards of the manifold grace of God, we will give an account of that for which we have responsibility. It is our responsibility to study and become an approved workman who rightly divides the word, who responds to the call, and who operates in the gifting of the grace of God. If we are not allowing God to work the gifts through us, we are not fulfilling our function in the body the Christ.

We see the Unity of the Father, the Son, and the Spirit in the will, in the gifting of God and the working of God. Jesus did not begin to minister until he had received the power of the Holy Spirit. After his temptation in the wilderness, he began to preach and to work miracles as his Father taught him. Jesus said I don't do anything but what I see the Father do. He showed Jesus what to do and say by the Holy Spirit just like he shows us who believe. We have a measure of the Spirit which operates in each of us individually and corporately, but Jesus was not given the Spirit by measure (Joh 3:34). He operated in the fullness of the Spirit's wisdom and power. We can only come to that perfect man in Christ through the unity of the body of Christ in faith and knowledge of Christ. We are one part of many in the body which are necessary to promote the preaching and teaching of the gospel of the kingdom of God. It is therefore critical that we seek and receive from God the calling and gifting of the Holy Spirit that we might function in the body according to the will of God. As the Father loved Jesus, he loves us and will show us greater works than we have experienced. Jesus said he that believes on him would do greater works than he did. So be it to us according to your will Father. Let us be about our Father's business as Jesus was. Oh Father, make us good stewards of all you have given us and work your works in and through us in the name of your Holy Son Jesus.

Joh 5:17 But Jesus answered them, My Father worketh hitherto, and I work.

Joh 5:18 Therefore the Jews sought the more to kill him, because he not only had broken the sabbath, but said also that God was his Father, making himself equal with God.

Joh 5:19 Then answered Jesus and said unto them, Verily, verily, I say unto you, The Son can do nothing of himself, but what he seeth the Father do: for what things soever he doeth, these also doeth the Son likewise.

Joh 5:20 For the Father loveth the Son, and sheweth him all things that himself doeth: and he will shew him greater works than these, that ye may marvel.

Joh 14:10 Believest thou not that I am in the Father, and the Father in me? the words that I speak unto you I speak not of myself: but **the Father that dwelleth in me, he doeth the works.**

Joh 14:11 Believe me that I am in the Father, and the Father in me: or else believe me for the very works' sake.

Joh 14:12 Verily, verily, I say unto you, **He that believeth on me, the works that I do shall he do also; and greater works** than these shall he do; because I go unto my Father.

MINISTER THE SPIRIT BY HEARING

Gal 3:5 He therefore that ministereth to you the Spirit, and worketh miracles among you, *doeth he it* by the works of the law, or by the **hearing of faith?**

Joh 5:19 Then answered Jesus and said unto them, Verily, verily, I say unto you, The Son **can do nothing of himself,** but what **he seeth** the Father do: for what things soever he doeth, these also doeth the Son likewise.

If we are to minister the Spirit to others and work miracles, it must be by the hearing of faith even as Jesus ministered. Whatever Jesus saw his father do, he did, and whatever his father told him to say, he said (Joh 5:19; Joh 12:49). Let us become honorable vessels and learn to listen to the Spirit that we might work such works of God.

> **1Co 12:27** Now ye are the body of Christ, and members in particular.
>
> **1Co 12:28** And God hath set some in the church, first apostles, secondarily prophets, thirdly teachers, after that miracles, then gifts of healings, helps, governments, diversities of tongues.
>
> **1Co 12:29** *Are* all apostles? *are* all prophets? *are* all teachers? *are* all workers of miracles?
>
> **1Co 12:30** Have all the gifts of healing? do all speak with tongues? do all interpret?
>
> **1Co 12:31** But **covet earnestly the best gifts**: and yet shew I unto you a more excellent way.

A servant of God motivated by love is going to seek the gifts that profit others and not seek honor from men. Before true greatness, there is humility before God and man. That means doing what we are told in obedience to his charge, not for profit but because of love. Jesus said, if you love me you will keep my commandments. Love is the fruit of the Spirit of God, and his love is shed abroad in our hearts if we are his. These gifts are not meant to exalt man but God by revealing his righteousness, his love, and his mercy for His people.

LESSON 13

Called to the Battle

OBJECTIVE: To establish and demonstrate an understanding of Spiritual Warfare.

SOLDIER OF CHRIST

2Ti 2:1   Thou therefore, my son, **be strong in the grace** that is in Christ Jesus.

2Ti 2:2   And the things that thou hast heard of me among many witnesses, the same commit thou to faithful men, who shall be able to teach others also.

2Ti 2:3   Thou therefore **endure hardness, as a good soldier of Jesus Christ.**

2 Ti 2:4   No man that warreth entangleth himself with the affairs of *this* life; that he may please him who hath chosen him to be a soldier.

God's grace has provided for everything we need, and that is where our strength lies. We have the assurance that his grace is sufficient for us and we know him who has called us to his side and equipped us to fight. A soldier knows there will be trouble and keeps himself fit for battle. The enemy will surely attack, and we cannot afford to be worldly-minded if we want to win the fight. Christ has already won the war against the works of the flesh and his spiritual rival, the devil, so let us manifest Christ victory in our lives and please him that has chosen us.

2Co 3:4   And such trust have we through Christ to God-ward:

2Co 3:5   Not that we are sufficient of ourselves to think any thing as of ourselves; but our sufficiency *is* of God.

THE WAR AGAINST THE SOUL

1Pe 2:11   Dearly beloved, I beseech *you* as strangers and pilgrims, **abstain from fleshly lusts, which war against the soul;**

1Pe 2:12   Having your conversation honest among the Gentiles: that, whereas they speak against you as evildoers, they may by *your* good works, which they shall behold, glorify God in the day of visitation.

2Co 10:3   For though we walk in the flesh, **we do not war after the flesh:**

2Co 10:4   (For the weapons of our warfare *are* not carnal, but mighty through God to the pulling down of strong holds;)

2Co 10:5 Casting down imaginations, and every high thing that exalteth itself against the knowledge of God, and **bringing into captivity every thought** to the obedience of Christ;

Peter tells us to abstain from carnal lusts because they battle against our soul's best interest (1Pe 2:11). This warfare takes place in our minds, and we are to be actively engaged in it by casting down imaginations, capturing our thoughts and bringing them under Christ control. Bringing our thoughts under the obedience of Christ requires bringing the cutting edge of the sword of the Spirit into play to cut away the fleshly mind. Jesus is our example to follow, and he used the word of God when tempted by evil. The Word of God is the lamp that lights our way in this world, and it is the standard of truth by which all shall be judged. When we accept the word of God as the standard of truth, we are open to receive discernment and instruction in righteous judgment.

Heb 4:12 For the word of God *is* quick, and powerful, and sharper than any two-edged sword, piercing even to the dividing asunder of soul and spirit, and of the joints and marrow, and *is* **a discerner of the thoughts and intents of the heart.**

Act 20:32 And now, brethren, I commend you to God, and to the word of his grace, which is able to build you up, and to give you an inheritance among all them which are sanctified.

THE LORD OF HOSTS

Eph 6:10 Finally, my brethren, **be strong in the Lord,** and in the power of his might.

Eph 6:11 Put on the whole armour of God, that ye may be able to stand against the wiles of the devil.

Eph 6:12 For we wrestle not against flesh and blood, but against principalities, against powers, against the rulers of the darkness of this world, against spiritual wickedness in high places.

The armor of God is an armor of light and an armor of righteousness Rom13:12; 2 Cor 6:7. To wear the armor we must cast off the works of darkness and be clothed with the righteousness of God's son.

Rom 13:12 The night is far spent, the day is at hand: let us therefore cast off the works of darkness, and let us put on **the armour of light.**

2Co 6:7 By the word of truth, by the power of God, by the **armour of righteousness** on the right hand and on the left.

The principalities are the chief ranking demonic beings/devils in the kingdom of darkness. The powers are lower ranking forces which have delegated authority or jurisdiction of certain areas. That could explain why Legion did not want to leave that country (Mar 5:9-10). These powers are delegated authorities of a particular region by the devil who is the god of this world. He is the chief of all principalities and powers of darkness. When Daniel prayed for understanding, God sent him Gabriel who was withstood by the Prince of Persia until Michael the Archangel came to help. It took him twenty-one days to break through the demonic stronghold. Michael was met by the chief principality of darkness that ruled over Persia (Dan 10:12-13). So it is with all countries, except those who acknowledge Jesus as their Lord and King. Daniel was a significant player in that nation, a trusted wise man in the courts of the King of Persia. The demonic forces of that region would come under the authority of the Prince of Persia as soldiers for battle.

Michael the archangel is the Chief Prince of the angels under Jesus who is Captain of the Hosts of the LORD. Our LORD is a man of war.

Exo 15:2 The LORD (Jah) *is* my strength and song, and he is become my **salvation:** he *is* my God, and I will prepare him an habitation; my father's God, and I will exalt him.

Exo 15:3 The LORD (the Eternal) *is* **a man of war: the LORD (Jehovah)** *is* **his name.**

Jos 5:13 And it came to pass, when Joshua was by Jericho, that he lifted up his eyes and looked, and, behold, there stood a man over against him with his sword drawn in his hand: and Joshua went unto him, and said unto him, *Art* thou for us, or for our adversaries?

Jos 5:14 And he said, Nay; but *as* **captain of the host of the LORD** am I now come. And Joshua fell on his face to the earth, and did **worship**, and said unto him, What saith my lord unto his servant?

Jos 5:15 And the captain of the LORD'S host said unto Joshua, Loose thy shoe from off thy foot; for **the place whereon thou standest** *is* **holy.** And Joshua did so.

Jah who is my strength and song has become my salvation. We know him as Jesus which means God is my salvation (Mat 1:21). The self-existent, eternal God is a man of war and Jehovah is his name. Jehovah is the national name of the God of Israel. The same LORD, the man of war lives inside our temple which has become a habitation of God through the Spirit and the place we stand is holy ground. It is he who is the higher power and has the greater mind who is in us than he who is in the world. Worship the LORD GOD and receive instruction and be empowered with his strength in his holy presence. He is present to direct the battle and enable his own army for victory.

THE SPIRITS ARE SUBJECT TO US

> 1Jn 4:4 Ye are of God, little children, and **have overcome them: because greater is he that is in you,** than he that is in the world.

As soldiers of the cross, we are engaging in spiritual warfare, not against men but evil spirits in the kingdom of darkness. The armor of God is an armor of light (Rom 13:12). Light expels the darkness. We are told to be strong in Jesus and the dominion of his ability and force. We have power over all the dominion of the enemy.

We have power over all his kingdom because one greater than him stripped him of his authority and triumphed over him in it. The church is to demonstrate the wisdom of God to these principalities and powers by exercising Christ authority over them. We are in Christ the greater one and walk in his delegated authority and power. In the Old Testament, men had authority and power in the Spirit when God's anointing came upon them. Now the anointing lives within the believer. David, a musician, played under the anointing and the devil departed.

> 1Sa 16:23 And it came to pass, when the *evil* spirit from God was upon Saul, that **David took an harp, and played** with his hand: so Saul was refreshed, and was well, **and the evil spirit departed** from him.

> **Luk 10:17** And the seventy returned again with joy, saying, Lord, even the devils are subject unto us through thy name.

Luk 10:18 And he said unto them, I beheld Satan as lightning fall from heaven.

Luk 10:19 Behold, **I give unto you power** to tread on serpents and scorpions, and **over all the power of the enemy**: and nothing shall by any means hurt you.

Luk 10:20 Notwithstanding in this rejoice not, that **the spirits are subject unto you;** but rather rejoice, because your names are written in heaven.

Luk 10:21 In that hour Jesus rejoiced in spirit, and said, I thank thee, O Father, Lord of heaven and earth, that thou hast hid these things from the wise and prudent, and hast revealed them unto babes: even so, Father; for so it seemed good in thy sight.

Eph 3:9 And to make all *men* see what *is* the fellowship of the mystery, which from the beginning of the world hath been hid in God, who created all things by Jesus Christ:

Eph 3:10 To the intent that now **unto the principalities and powers** in heavenly *places* **might be known by the church** the manifold wisdom of God.

Col 2:14 Blotting out the handwriting of ordinances that was against us, which was contrary to us, and took it out of the way, nailing it to his cross;

Col 2:15 *And* having **spoiled principalities and powers,** he made a shew of them openly, triumphing over them in it.

Christ Jesus spoiled the principalities and powers through his death and resurrection by bringing down the strongman who ruled over them. When he raised from the dead, he had the keys of death and hell, having conquered both (Rev 1:18). At that time when a conqueror came home from battle victorious, he would parade the enemy bound and naked before all the people and receive acclamations of praise from his people. Jesus did likewise to the devil and his demons by stripping them of power and proclaiming his authority and power before all the angels and people of heaven and earth. That authority is exercised today by the church, and his glory shown to the principalities in the heavenly places as we stand in Christ power and reign over them.

Eph 1:17 That the God of our Lord Jesus Christ, the Father of glory, may give unto you the spirit of wisdom and revelation in the knowledge of him:

Eph 1:18 The eyes of your understanding being enlightened; that ye may know what is the hope of his calling, and what the riches of the glory of his inheritance in the saints.

Eph 1:19 And what *is* the exceeding greatness of his power to us-ward who believe, according to the working of his mighty power.

Eph 1:20 Which he wrought in Christ, when he raised him from the dead, and **set *him* at his own right hand in the heavenly *places.***

Eph 1:21 **Far above all principality, and power, and might, and dominion, and every name that is named,** not only in this world, but also in that which is to come:

Eph 1:22 And **hath put all *things* under his feet,** and gave him *to be* the head over all *things* to the church.

Eph 1:23   Which is his body, the fulness of him that filleth all in all.

TRY THE SPIRITS

Satan is a master at illusion and deceit. He can transform himself into an angel of light. His ministers also appear as ministers of righteousness.

2Co 11:13   For such *are* false apostles, deceitful workers, transforming themselves into the apostles of Christ.

2Co 11:14   And no marvel; for **Satan himself is transformed into an angel of light.**

2Co 11:15   Therefore *it is* **no great thing if his ministers also be transformed** as the ministers of righteousness; whose end shall be according to their works.

SATAN—THE DEVIL / DEMON

- he is the serpent (artful, malicious)— (Gen 3:1 ; Rev 20:2)
- he is the tempter—(Mat 4:3; 1Th 3:5)
- he is the accuser/slanderer of the brethren—(Rev 12:10)
- he is a liar and the father of lies—(Joh 8:44)
- he is a murderer—(Joh 8:44)
- he is a thief/comes to steal, kill, and destroy—(Joh 10:10)
- he is a deceiver—beguiler—(Gen 3:13)
- he is like a roaring lion seeking whom he may devour—(1Pe 5:8)

- he is the great red dragon—(Rev 12:3)
- he is the god of this world—(2Co 4:4)
- he is prince of the power of the air—(Eph 2:2)

Satan would love to steal from the church the doctrine of the incarnation of the Son of God because he knows that Christ is the only hope of the world. He provides men with doctrines of demons which tickle their ears and leads them to hell. Some insist that God does not have a son and so it is with many false religions of the world. They deny the Son of God. John by the Spirit warns us about false prophets and their doctrine. He exhorts us to test or try the spirits to see whether they are really from God. If they do not bring the doctrine of the Son of God Incarnate, they are that spirit of antichrist.

> 1Jn 4:1 Beloved, believe not every spirit, but **try the spirits** whether they are of God: because many false prophets are gone out into the world.
>
> 1Jn 4:2 Hereby know ye the Spirit of God: Every spirit that confesseth that Jesus Christ is come in the flesh is of God:
>
> 1Jn 4:3 **And every spirit that confesseth not that Jesus Christ is come in the flesh is not of God: and this is that *spirit* of antichrist,** whereof ye have heard that it should come; and even now already is it in the world.
>
> 1Jn 4:4 Ye are of God, little children, and have overcome them: because **greater is he that is in you,** than he that is in the world.
>
> 1Jn 4:5 They are of the world: therefore **speak they of the world**, and the world heareth them.

1Jn 5:11 And this is the record, that God hath given to us eternal life, and this life is in his Son.

1Jn 5:12 He that hath the Son hath life; *and* he that hath not the Son of God hath not life.

Jesus Christ is the Word who became flesh (Joh 1:1-3,14). Whoever does not believe and confess this doctrine and does not abide in the doctrine of Christ and the Apostles is not of God but the world. We have overcome those lying spirits because greater is he that is in us than he that is in the world. The spirit of antichrist is in the world and many false prophets who deny that Christ came in the flesh. They want to make him into their image instead of believing what He said about himself. He proclaimed to the Pharisees that he was the Son sent from above and that if they do not believe, they will die in their sins. Those who reject Christ claims are from the spirit of antichrist, and they shall die in their sins, unforgiven.

Joh 1:1 In the beginning was the Word, and **the Word was with God,** and the **Word was God.**

Joh 1:2 The same was **in the beginning with God.**

Joh 1:3 All things were made by him; and without him was not any thing made that was made.

Joh 1:4 In him was life; and the life was the light of men.

Joh 1:14 And **the Word was made flesh**, and dwelt among us, (and we beheld his glory, the glory as of the only begotten of the Father,) full of grace and truth.

Joh 1:15 John bare witness of him, and cried, saying, This was he of whom I spake, He that cometh after me is preferred before me: for **he was before me.**

Joh 3:31 He that cometh from above is above all: he that is of the earth is earthly, and speaketh of the earth: **he that cometh from heaven** is above all.

Joh 8:23 And he said unto them, Ye are from beneath; **I am from above:** ye are of this world; **I am not of this world.**

Joh 8:24 I said therefore unto you, that ye shall die in your sins: for if ye believe not that I am *he,* ye shall die in your sins.

The prophets witness that God has a son and that he would send him from heaven. He would be called Immanuel, God with us, born of a virgin, and his name would be called Wonderful, Counsellor, The Mighty God, the Everlasting Father, the Prince of Peace. John the Baptist bore witness that Jesus existed before him and that he is the one sent from heaven. His name represents all he is, and in Christ, we carry the power and the authority of that great name representing the Kingdom of God.

Isa 7:14 Therefore the Lord himself shall give you a sign; Behold, **a virgin** shall conceive, and bear a son, and shall call **his name Immanuel.**

Isa 9:6 For unto us a child is born, unto us **a son is given**: and the government shall be upon his shoulder: and his name shall be called Wonderful, Counsellor, The mighty God, The everlasting Father, The Prince of Peace.

Isa 9:7 Of the increase of *his* **government and peace there shall be** **no end,** upon the throne of David, and upon his kingdom, to order it, and to establish it with judgment and with justice from henceforth even for ever. The zeal of the LORD of hosts will perform this.

Jesus shared glory with his Father God before he came to earth to become flesh in the womb of a virgin. He was not an angel nor any created being. He was the creator himself, the Word of God who created all things with his Father. In (Isa 48:16) the one who is the first and the last says, the Lord GOD and his Spirit hath sent me. Here is the triune God before the incarnation of Christ. The Father Jehovah and his Spirit sent the Son Jehovah and he became flesh and was named Jesus because he would save his people from their sins. Jesus means God is our Salvation.

Exo 15:2 **The LORD** (Jah) *is* my strength and song, and **he is become my salvation:** he *is* my God, and I will prepare him an habitation; my father's God, and I will exalt him.

Exo 15:3 **The LORD** (the Eternal) *is* a man of war: the **LORD (Jehovah)** *is* his name.

Isa 48:12 Hearken unto me, O Jacob and Israel, my called; I *am* he; **I *am* the first, I also *am* the last.**

Isa 48:13 Mine hand also hath laid the foundation of the earth, and my right hand hath spanned the heavens: *when* I call unto them, they stand up together.

Rev 1:8 I am Alpha and Omega, the beginning and the ending, saith the Lord, which is, and which was, and which is to come, the Almighty.

Rev 1:17 And when I saw him, I fell at his feet as dead. And he laid his right hand upon me, saying unto me, Fear not; **I am the first and the last:**

Rev 1:18 *I am* he that liveth, and was dead; and, behold, I am alive for evermore, Amen; and have the keys of hell and of death.

Pro 30:4 Who hath ascended up into heaven, or descended? who hath gathered the wind in his fists? who hath bound the waters in a garment? who hath established all the ends of the earth? **what** *is* **his name,** and **what** *is* **his son's name,** if thou canst tell?

God gives us a riddle to solve, and the answer is Jehovah for both. Jesus was in the form, the shape, the nature of God before he came to earth.

Php 2:6 Who, being **in the form of God**, thought it not robbery to be equal with God:

Php 2:7 But **made himself of no reputation, and took upon him the form of a servant,** and was made in the likeness of men:

Php 2:8 And being found in fashion as a man, he humbled himself, and became obedient unto death, even the death of the cross.

Php 2:9 Wherefore God also hath highly exalted him, and given him a **name which is above every name:**

Php 2:10 That at the name of Jesus every knee should bow, of *things* in heaven, and *things* in earth, and *things* under the earth;

Php 2:11 And *that* **every tongue should confess that Jesus Christ *is* Lord,** to the glory of God the Father.

Isa 48:16 Come ye near unto me, hear ye this; I have not spoken in secret from the beginning; from the time that it was, there *am* I: and now **the Lord GOD, and his Spirit, hath sent me.**

Man was trapped in sin and death and could not ascend to heaven, and that is why Christ descended from Heaven; to be the way. Jesus was sent from above to do the Father's will. Before he came to earth, he was in the form of God, and he was not robbing his Father of any glory by considering himself equal to him (Php 2). He humbled himself and took on the form of a servant, becoming flesh, and he was obedient unto death that he might save humanity from his sins. When Jesus was baptized, the Holy Spirit descended like a dove upon him and abode there, and his Father spoke from heaven bearing witness of his son. Here again, we see the Triune God, the Godhead, revealed as a relationship between Father, Son, and Holy Spirit. Jesus is the object of the Father's love and pleasure. They share the glory of the Godhead.

Isa 45:21 Tell ye, and bring *them* near; yea, let them take counsel together: who hath declared this from ancient time? *who* hath told it from that time? *have* not I the LORD? and *there is* no God else beside me; a just God and a **Saviour;** *there is* none beside me.

Isa 45:22 Look unto me, and be ye saved, all the ends of the earth: for I *am* God, and *there is* none else.

Isa 45:23 I have sworn by myself, the word is gone out of my mouth *in* righteousness, and shall not return, That **unto me every knee shall bow, every tongue shall swear.**

Isa 45:24 Surely, shall *one* say, in the LORD have I righteousness and strength: *even* to him shall *men* come; and all that are incensed against him shall be ashamed.

Isa 45:25 In the LORD shall all the seed of Israel be justified, and shall glory.

Col 2:8 Beware lest any man spoil you through philosophy and vain deceit, after the tradition of men, after the rudiments of the world, and not after Christ.

Col 2:9 For in him dwelleth all the fulness of the Godhead bodily.

Joh 3:18 He that believeth on him is not condemned: but he that believeth not is condemned already, because he hath not believed in the **name of the only begotten.**

LESSON 14

The Armor of God

OBJECTIVE: To develop and demonstrate an understanding of the Armor of God.

OUR ENEMY HAS HAD THOUSANDS OF YEARS TO hone his skills, and he is cunning and malicious. Only in Christ armor can we battle him with success. Learning how to be strong in the Lord and his might is a matter of training. Just as a soldier must learn how to use his equipment, so we should learn all about the armor God has given us. Each piece is representative of Christ himself. Knowing that Christ has already defeated our enemy is key to becoming victorious in each battle. That is why we are to be strong in him, his power and his might. He has already prevailed and clothed with his armor, so shall we.

> Eph 6:10   Finally, my brethren, be strong in the Lord, and in the power of his might.

> Eph 6:11   Put on the **whole armour of God,** that ye may be able to stand against the wiles of the devil.

Eph 6:12 For we wrestle not against flesh and blood, but against principalities, against powers, against the rulers of the darkness of this world, against spiritual wickedness in high places.

Eph 6:13 Wherefore take unto you **the whole armour of God,** that ye may be able to withstand in the evil day, and having done all, to stand.

Eph 6:14 Stand therefore, having your loins girt about with truth, and having on the breastplate of righteousness;

Eph 6:15 And your feet shod with the preparation of the gospel of peace;

Eph 6:16 Above all, taking the shield of faith, wherewith ye shall be able to quench all the fiery darts of the wicked.

Eph 6:17 And take the helmet of salvation, and the sword of the Spirit, which is the word of God:

Eph 6:18 Praying always with all prayer and supplication in the Spirit, and watching thereunto with all perseverance and supplication for all saints;

The whole armor of God is an armor of truth and righteousness and faith in Christ Jesus. We must take it unto us, protecting ourselves against the demonic attack of our minds and hearts. Therefore we are to put on the whole armor from head to foot. It begins with having an intimate knowledge of Jesus who is the truth. The offensive weapons of the armor are the sword of the Spirit and the shield of faith.

GIRDLE OF TRUTH

Eph 6:14 Stand therefore, having your **loins girt about with truth**, and having on the breastplate of righteousness;

- loins—the hip, procreative power.

Joh 14:6 Jesus saith unto him, I am the way, **the truth,** and the life: no man cometh unto the Father, but by me.

This piece of the armor, the truth, is that which strengthens our frame by wrapping tightly around the loins. Girt means to fasten on one's belt. We are counted to Jesus as his seed, and we have no life but through him. He is our connection to God through the Spirit. The revelation of this truth is the foundation of the armor. To the girdle is connected the breastplate of righteousness and the scabbard with the sword of the Spirit. The Holy Spirit of Truth has been sent to reveal Jesus and guide us into all truth.

BREASTPLATE OF RIGHTEOUSNESS

Eph 6:14 Stand therefore, having your loins girt about with truth, and having on the **breastplate of righteousness**;

We are made righteous in Christ Jesus; therefore He is our breastplate. There is no condemnation to those who are in Christ Jesus. We have been made righteous freely by his grace.

Rom 3:21 But now **the righteousness of God** without the law is manifested, being witnessed by the law and the prophets;

Rom 3:22 Even the **righteousness of God** *which is* **by faith of Jesus Christ unto all and upon all them that believe:** for there is no difference:

Rom 3:23 For all have sinned, and come short of the glory of God;

Rom 3:24 Being justified freely by his grace through the redemption that is in Christ Jesus:

Rom 3:25 Whom God hath set forth *to be* a propitiation through faith in his blood, **to declare his righteousness** for the remission of sins that are past, through the forbearance of God;

Rom 3:26 **To declare,** *I say,* **at this time his righteousness:** that he might be just, and **the justifier of him which believeth** in Jesus.

Rom 3:27 Where *is* boasting then? It is excluded. By what law? of works? Nay: but by the law of faith.

Rom 3:28 Therefore we conclude that a man is justified by faith without the deeds of the law.

Jesus is the justifier which means he makes us righteous before God.

Rom 5:17 For if by one man's offence death reigned by one; much more they which receive abundance of grace and of the gift of righteousness shall reign in life by one, Jesus Christ.)

It is through Christ abundance of grace and the gift of righteousness that we reign in life. That means we live victorious over the flesh and the enemy. We cannot approach the enemy in our righteousness for his wiles and weapons of condemnation will enter our hearts and rob us of our confidence. We cannot attain to the righteousness of the law, but Christ did, and we are in him through faith. We have no reason nor right to boast of our works because we are justified only through the Law of Faith (Rom 3:27). Jesus has given us his righteousness which protects our hearts like a breastplate of armor against the accusations and torments of the enemy. Imagine if we had to wear a breastplate of our righteousness. Our righteousness is as an unclean thing, a filthy rag (Isa 64:4). Jesus righteousness is pristine and pure in holiness and splendor. It is God's righteousness that we preach, not our own.

> Php 3:9   And be found in him, **not having mine own righteousness,** which is of the law, but that which is through the faith of Christ, the righteousness which is of God by faith:

PREPARATION OF THE GOSPEL OF PEACE

> Eph 6:15   And your feet shod with the preparation of the gospel of peace;

> Eph 2:13   But now in Christ Jesus ye who sometimes were far off are made nigh by the blood of Christ.

> Eph 2:14   For **he is our peace**, who hath made both one, and hath broken down the middle wall of partition *between us;*

We have been made near to God by the blood of Jesus who has made us one through faith in him. God has torn down all walls and prejudices by Christ Jesus who bore our chastisement thereby making peace, reconciling us with God. We can now walk in peace/ union with God and all who abide in Christ. Trusting God with our lives and being ready to preach the gospel of peace to every creature we stand in this grace and this world as a new creation; in the world but not of the world. We stand as an overcomer against our enemy by the blood of the lamb and the word of our testimony (Rev 12:11). Jesus lived, suffered, and died and rose from the dead three days later appearing before the Father with the atonement for our sins so we now might walk in peace/union with God and man.

Rom 5:1   Therefore being justified by faith, we have **peace with God** through our Lord Jesus Christ:

Rom 5:2   By whom also we have access by faith **into this grace wherein we stand**, and rejoice in hope of the glory of God.

SHIELD OF FAITH

Eph 6:16   Above all, taking the **shield of faith**, wherewith ye shall be able to quench all the fiery darts of the wicked.

Pro 30:5   Every word of God *is* pure: **he *is* a shield** unto them that put their trust in him.

Men of God have learned through the ages that God is their shield and their refuge. He is a present help in time of need; the shield of our help (Deu 33:29). The LORD told Abraham that He was his shield and his exceeding great reward (Gen 15:1).

The shield of Ephesians 6 is a large shield-shaped much like a door. It is meant to protect the whole man. Above all, we hold up the shield of faith which protects us during warfare. Like David when he came against Goliath, we run at the enemy in the name of the LORD of Hosts and through faith in his name we bring down the enemy. Our shield, our protection is in the name of our God, the Man of War, The LORD of Hosts (Exo 15:3). We fight the good fight of faith in Jesus name and make our stand on God's word. In Acts 3:16 Peter said that the lame man was healed by Jesus name, through faith in his name. The Psalmist said in (Psa 44:5-8) that we tread down our enemies through God's name and in his name we boast. There is power in the name of Jesus. The enemy knows we have the upper hand in the battle but do we?

> **Luk 10:19** Behold, **I give unto you power** to tread on serpents and scorpions, and **over all the power of the enemy**: and nothing shall by any means hurt you.

The shield of faith is Jesus himself in whom we dwell in the Spirit. Our trust is not in ourselves but the strength of the name of the Lord and the power of his might. He is our shield, and he has given us the power to tread on all the power of the enemy by exercising the dominion he has given us over all principalities and powers. We do this by calling on Christ Jesus name, thereby calling on the resources of his kingdom of light. Nothing shall by any means hurt us because we have a shield and the enemy's fiery darts cannot penetrate him.

HELMET OF SALVATION

> **Eph 6:17** And take the **helmet of salvation**, and the sword of the Spirit, which is the word of God:

> **Exo 15:2** The LORD (Jah) *is* my strength and song, and **he is become my salvation: he *is* my God,** and I will prepare him an habitation; my father's God, and I will exalt him.

The Lord Jesus has become our salvation, and he is our God. His helmet protects our mind against the onslaught of demonic forces trying to take over our thoughts.

We have the mind of Christ and a spirit of power, love and a sound mind. The god of this world, Satan has blinded the minds of those who do not believe, and they walk in darkness. His influence is apparent in all cultures of the world for the whole world lies captive under his power. It is into this battle fray we are called to be a light and to reach the souls of men. It is imperative that our minds are trained to reason and judge by the Spirit of the Living God. Knowledge of Christ is our Helmet. The Lord Jesus has become our salvation and he is our God. His helmet protects our mind against the onslaught of demonic forces trying to take over our thoughts. God instructs us to remember that we are spiritual and able to judge all things. Therefore it is essential to stir up the gift of God in us by worship and prayer and to sit at Jesus' feet learning his word.

> **1Co 2:15** But he that is spiritual judgeth all things, yet he himself is judged of no man.
>
> **1Co 2:16** For who hath known the mind of the Lord, that he may instruct him? But **we have the mind of Christ.**
>
> **2Ti 1:6** Wherefore I put thee in remembrance that thou stir up the gift of God, which is in thee by the putting on of my hands.
>
> **2Ti 1:7** For God hath not given us the spirit of fear; but of power, and of love, and of **a sound mind.**

Allowing the Holy Spirit to teach us God's word as we fellowship daily is arming our minds with light, with soundness. We have the mind of Christ, and his mind is sound. The salvation of Christ is altogether past, present, and future. Delivered from sin and death through Christ sacrifice, we experience daily the blessings of his salvation. We live in the hope of everlasting life for our souls for we are not appointed to receive the wrath of God. At Christ revelation, the believer will experience change into incorruptible perfection of his mind and body in the twinkling of an eye and shall be presented blameless before the Father (1 Co 15:50-54, 1 Th 3:13).

1Th 5:8   But let us, who are of the day, be sober, putting on the breastplate of faith and love; and for an **helmet, the hope of salvation.**

1Th 5:9   For God hath not appointed us to wrath, but to obtain **salvation by our Lord Jesus Christ.**

1Pe 1:7   That the trial of your faith, being much more precious than of gold that perisheth, though it be tried with fire, might be found unto praise and honour and glory **at the appearing of Jesus Christ:**

1Pe 1:8   Whom having not seen, ye love; in whom, though now ye see *him* not, yet believing, ye rejoice with joy unspeakable and full of glory:

1Pe 1:9   Receiving the **end of your faith,** *even* the **salvation** of *your* souls.

SWORD OF THE SPIRIT

Eph 6:17   And take the helmet of salvation, and **the sword of the Spirit, which is the word of God:**

Eph 6:18   Praying always with all prayer and supplication in the Spirit, and watching thereunto with all perseverance and supplication for all saints;

Praying God's word is praying spiritual prayers by bringing his promises before him and laying claim to them through faith. We are to persevere in prayer staying alert and applying our faith until the answer promised is manifested.

Jesus showed us how to fight with the sword of the Spirit. When he was faced with temptation from the devil he used the Word of God in response. The sword is an offensive weapon to use against our enemy (Luk 4). It is a sword of light, for the word is a light that scatters the darkness.

All parts of the armor represent Christ and his power by which he defeated the devil for us. In a confrontation with the Pharisees and Sadducees about his teachings he confounded them with his wisdom and knowledge of the scriptures. They could not dispute the power and the wisdom of his words.

When we wield this sword, our enemy flees. His gates of hell are defenseless against the church, and his weapons of warfare are not effective against us when we make our stand. Christ has already stormed the gates of hell and given us the authority to do the same. With his word, he cast out devils, healed the sick and raised the dead and by the power of Holy Spirit, we can do the same using Christ authority, his armor, his word, and his name.

We have the authority to bind and to let loose. The kingdom of God allows violence against the powers of darkness and the violent take the kingdom by force from him. When we pray we become violent in the fight because it is a fight for life for those who cannot fight themselves. Jesus has already bound the strongman and give us power over him. He spoke the word and cast out devils and so can we.

Mat 12:28 But if **I cast out devils by the Spirit of God,** then the kingdom of God is come unto you.

Mat 12:29 Or else how can one enter into a strong man's house, and spoil his goods, except he first bind the strong man? and then he will spoil his house.

The violence against Satan's kingdom began at the preaching of John. He came as the forerunner to Christ to prepare the way of the Lord. Shortly after John began preaching and baptizing, Jesus came on the scene. He conquered temptation in the wilderness and put the devil under his feet. He came back from the desert victorious and began to wreak havoc on Satan's kingdom. God suffers/allows us to be violent when addressing the devil. Warfare is violence against the kingdom of darkness.

Mat 11:12 And from the days of John the Baptist until now the kingdom of heaven suffereth violence, and the violent take it by force.

LESSON 15

The Watchman

OBJECTIVE: To learn and develop the discipline of watching and praying.

IN THIS CHAPTER, THERE IS A REMINDER OF what will keep us through all manner of trial we face in this world as we watch for the Master's return. We are also reminded to obey Christ commandments to love one another in sincerity and truth, forgiving and praying for one another so that Satan does not get an advantage over us.

WATCH AND PRAY

Eph 6:18 Praying always with all prayer and supplication in the Spirit, and **watching** thereunto with all perseverance and supplication for all saints;

- watch—keep awake, be vigilant.

1Pe 4:7 But **the end of all things is at hand**: be ye therefore sober, and **watch unto prayer.**

1Pe 4:8 And above all things have fervent charity among yourselves: for charity shall cover the multitude of sins.

1Co 13:1 Though I speak with the tongues of men and of angels, and have not **charity**, I am become *as* sounding brass, or a tinkling cymbal.

1Co 13:2 And though I have *the gift of* prophecy, and understand all mysteries, and all knowledge; and though I have all faith, so that I could remove mountains, and have not **charity**, I am nothing.

Paul reminds us that even if we speak many languages including that of angels but we do not love we are just making much noise that does not benefit the hearer. If we have a great understanding and all knowledge and faith that can remove mountains and do not have love we are nothing.

1Th 5:8 But let us, who are of the day, be sober, putting on the **breastplate of faith and love**; and for an helmet, the hope of salvation.

1Th 5:9 For God hath not appointed us to wrath, but to obtain salvation by our Lord Jesus Christ.

Joh 9:4 I must work the works of him that sent me, while it is day: the night cometh, when no man can work.

Joh 9:5 As long as I am in the world, I am the light of the world.

Col 4:5 Walk in wisdom toward them that are without, **redeeming the time.**

Col 4:6 Let your speech *be* alway with grace, seasoned with salt, that ye may know how ye ought to answer every man.

Pro 11:30 The fruit of the righteous *is* a tree of life; and **he that winneth souls *is* wise.**

To walk in wisdom is to walk in obedience to God's revealed word realizing that it is important to use time wisely for the night comes when no man can work. Like Jesus, we are the light of the world as long as we are in the world. We must stay alert, so the Day of the Lord does not take us unaware. We are to watch, pray, and take heed, so we do not enter into temptation. Do not be ignorant of Satan's devices. He appeals to the flesh and then he accuses and condemns the heart. He will cause us to think about evil if we do not guard our heart. Knowing that man's weakness is his flesh, the devil plants the seeds (thoughts) of wickedness and watches to see if we will receive it. Once he has us dwelling on the lusts of the flesh, he has us in his snare. That is why it is essential to learn to be vigilant and renew our minds. The devil wants to neutralize our effect in this world and keep us spiritually asleep. He will steal our time from the word of God and prayer, our necessary disciplines to build ourselves up to become mighty warriors in Christ. Our instructions are to take heed, watch and pray always that we may be accounted worthy to escape all the things coming upon the earth and to stand before Jesus the Judge.

Mat 26:41 **Watch and pray**, that ye enter not into temptation: the spirit indeed *is* willing, but the flesh *is* weak.

Luk 21:34 And **take heed** to yourselves, lest at any time your hearts be overcharged with surfeiting, and drunkenness, and cares of this life, and *so* **that day come upon you unawares.**

Luk 21:35   For as a snare shall it come on all them that dwell on the face of the whole earth.

Luk 21:36 **Watch ye therefore, and pray always,** that ye may be accounted worthy **to escape all these things that shall come to pass,** and to stand before the Son of man.

God does not want our hearts overburdened with the pain that comes from the lifestyle of the world and the stress of its consequences. We can become so carried away with worries and fears of this world that we lose sight of who our God is and what his word says. Jesus says not to worry about what we shall eat or drink or what we shall wear but to seek first his kingdom, and all things shall be provided for us (Mat 6:25-34). He instructs us to set our affection on things above not on the things of the earth (Col 3:1-6). If our hearts are after the things of the world instead of after the things of the Spirit of God, then we are not thinking soberly, and our adversary will get an advantage over us. God cares for us and exhorts us to cast all of our care upon him, to be sober and watchful in prayer and exercise control over the flesh as he instructs for we shall stand before God one day.

1Pe 5:6   Humble yourselves therefore under the mighty hand of God, that he may exalt you in due time:

1Pe 5:7   Casting all your care upon him; for he careth for you.

1Pe 5:8 Be sober, be vigilant; because your adversary the devil, as a roaring lion, walketh about, seeking whom he may devour:

1Pe 5:9 Whom **resist stedfast in the faith,** knowing that the same afflictions are accomplished in your brethren that are in the world.

1Pe 5:10 But the God of all grace, who hath called us unto his eternal glory by Christ Jesus, after that ye have suffered a while, make you perfect, stablish, strengthen, settle *you.*

1Pe 5:11 To him *be* glory and dominion for ever and ever. Amen.

The Church will suffer persecution and afflictions that the enemy stirs up against us. If we are alert, we will arm ourselves with a breastplate of faith and love and protect our minds with the hope of salvation.

When Christ appears we shall also appear with him in glory. That is our hope of salvation, our hope of glory when we shall be changed into Christ-likeness, from mortal to immortal, from corruptible to incorruptible. Therefore we are to be strong in faith and learn to cast all our cares upon him, who alone can help, and wait for the promise of his coming with faith and patience.

2Ti 4:1 I charge *thee* therefore before God, and the Lord Jesus Christ, who shall **judge the quick and the dead at his appearing** and his kingdom;

2Ti 4:2 **Preach the word;** be instant in season, out of season; reprove, rebuke, exhort with all longsuffering and doctrine.

2Ti 4:3 For the time will come when they will not endure **sound doctrine;** but after their own lusts shall they heap to themselves teachers, having itching ears;

2Ti 4:4   And they shall turn away *their* ears from the truth, and shall be turned unto fables.

2Ti 4:5   But **watch thou in all things**, endure afflictions, do the work of an evangelist, make full proof of thy ministry.

Those called to be ministers of the gospel are charged to preach the word of God, watch in all things, endure afflictions, evangelize and fulfill the ministry. All disciples are called to make a clean break from sin and carry out fully (make full proof of) the ministry God has entrusted and equipped them to accomplish. As children of light, our fellowship is with the Father and the Son, and we should have no association with darkness. We are encouraged to stay alert and pray in all manner of prayer in the Spirit. We can pray spiritual prayers in the tongues given through the baptism of the Holy Spirit or in our language. The tongue of the Holy Spirit can bypass our thinking which can limit God and takes us to the innermost recesses of the mind of God. He prays through us the prayers that need to be prayed on earth as we seek his help. God has given each of us authority and works to do according to how he has gifted. Let us watch and pray that when he comes, he finds us faithful.

1Th 5:1   But of the times and the seasons, brethren, ye have no need that I write unto you.

1Th 5:2   For yourselves know perfectly that **the day of the Lord so cometh** as a thief in the night.

1Th 5:3   For when they shall say, Peace and safety; then sudden destruction cometh upon them, as travail upon a woman with child; and they shall not escape.

1Th 5:4   **But ye, brethren, are not in darkness, that that day should overtake you as a thief.**

1Th 5:5 Ye are all the children of light, and the children of the day: we are not of the night, nor of darkness.

1Th 5:6 Therefore let us not sleep, as *do* others; but let us **watch and be sober.**

1Th 5:7 For they that sleep sleep in the night; and they that be drunken are drunken in the night.

Mar 13:32 But of that day and *that* hour knoweth no man, no, not the angels which are in heaven, neither the Son, but the Father.

Mar 13:33 **Take ye heed, watch and pray:** for ye know not when the time is.

Mar 13:34 *For the Son of man is* as a man taking a far journey, who left his house, and **gave authority to his servants, and to every man his work,** and commanded the porter to watch.

Mar 13:35 Watch ye therefore: for ye know not when the master of the house cometh, at even, or at midnight, or at the cockcrowing, or in the morning:

Mar 13:36 **Lest coming suddenly he find you sleeping.**

Mar 13:37 And what I say unto you I say unto all, **Watch.**

LESSON 16

Our Glorification

OBJECTIVE: To develop an understanding of our glorification at The Resurrection.

HOW ARE THE DEAD RAISED? WITH WHAT BODY?

1Co 15:35   But some *man* will say, How are the dead raised up? and with what body do they come?

1Co 15:36   *Thou* fool, that which thou sowest is not quickened, except it die:

1Co 15:37   And that which thou sowest, thou sowest not that body that shall be, but bare grain, it may chance of wheat, or of some other *grain:*

Just as grain such as wheat and corn have to die to rise up in a new body, even so, do we. When the seed is planted, it dies and then transforms into a new plant. So it will be with us. Our bodies, buried in corruption at death, are raised in incorruption at the resurrection. The body shall be changed and made glorious like our Lord's. Its glory is different from the old body which was corrupted and dead. It is transformed into a spiritual body, in beauty, in honor, and in power after the image of God's Son, never to experience sin and death again. We shall be forever free from any influence of evil.

1Co 15:38 But God giveth it a body as it hath pleased him, and to every seed his own body.

1Co 15:39 All flesh *is* not the same flesh: but *there is* one *kind of* flesh of men, another flesh of beasts, another of fishes, *and* another of birds.

1Co 15:40 *There are* also celestial bodies, and bodies terrestrial: but the glory of the celestial *is* one, and the *glory* of the terrestrial *is* another.

1Co 15:41 *There is* one glory of the sun, and another glory of the moon, and another glory of the stars: for *one* star differeth from *another* star in glory.

1Co 15:42 So also *is* the resurrection of the dead. It is sown in corruption; **it is raised in incorruption:**

1Co 15:43 It is sown in dishonour; **it is raised in glory**: it is sown in weakness; it is raised in power:

1Co 15:44 It is sown a natural body; it is raised a **spiritual body.** There is a natural body, and there is a spiritual body.

1Co 15:45 And so it is written, The first man Adam was made a living soul; **the last Adam** *was made* **a quickening spirit.**

1Co 15:46   Howbeit that *was* not first which is spiritual, but that which is natural; and afterward that which is spiritual.

1Co 15:47   The first man *is* of the earth, earthy: **the second man *is* the Lord from heaven.**

1Co 15:48   As *is* the earthy, such *are* they also that are earthy: and as *is* the heavenly, such *are* they also that are heavenly.

1Co 15:49   **And as we have borne the image of the earthy, we shall also bear the image of the heavenly.**

As the offspring of the first Adam we bare his image in our natural body, and as the offspring of the last Adam, we shall bear his image in our spiritual body. The spiritual body is not like the body that was planted at death yet the same body; resurrected and changed! It is spiritual flesh and bones, different from the natural flesh and blood man.

JESUS RESURRECTED BODY

When the disciples came to the tomb of Jesus, they found the stone rolled back from the entrance, and Jesus body gone. The angel of the Lord told them he was risen (Luk 24:1-12). Later he also appeared to two disciples on the road to Emmaus and conversed with them about his death and resurrection. They did not recognize him until He broke bread with them. He then disappeared right in front of their eyes and realizing who it was they hurried back to Jerusalem to tell the disciples (Luk 24:13-35). As they were speaking to the disciples, the Lord appeared in their midst.

Luk 24:36   And as they thus spake, Jesus himself stood in the midst of them, and saith unto them, Peace *be* unto you.

Luk 24:37   But they were terrified and affrighted, and **supposed that they had seen a spirit.**

Luk 24:38   And he said unto them, Why are ye troubled? and why do thoughts arise in your hearts?

Luk 24:39   **Behold my hands and my feet, that it is I myself: handle me, and see; for a spirit hath not flesh and bones, as ye see me have.**

Luk 24:40   And when he had thus spoken, he shewed them *his* hands and *his* feet.

Luk 24:41   And while they yet believed not for joy, and wondered, he said unto them, Have ye here any meat?

Luk 24:42   And they gave him a piece of a broiled fish, and of an honeycomb.

Luk 24:43   And **he took** *it,* **and did eat before them.**

Luk 24:44   And he said unto them, These *are* the words which I spake unto you, while I was yet with you, that all things must be fulfilled, which were written in the law of Moses, and *in* the prophets, and *in* the psalms, concerning me.

Luk 24:45   **Then opened he their understanding,** that they might understand the scriptures.

Luk 24:46   And said unto them, Thus it is written, and thus it behoved Christ to suffer, and to rise from the dead the third day:

Luk 24:47   And that repentance and remission of sins should be preached in his name among all nations, beginning at Jerusalem.

Luk 24:48   And ye are witnesses of these things.

Luk 24:49   And, behold, I send the promise of my Father upon you: but tarry ye in the city of Jerusalem, until ye be endued with power from on high.

The disciples were terrified when Jesus appeared in their midst although he addressed them with peace. They thought He was a spirit. Jesus made a statement which shows us something about his resurrected body. He said that he was not a spirit (ghost) because a spirit does not have flesh and bone as he had, then he ate some food. Jesus said he was flesh and bones, yet he can appear and disappear. We see here the spiritual body of flesh and bone spoken about in (1Co 15:44) This is the kind of body we shall have at the resurrection. The scripture teaches that flesh and blood cannot enter the kingdom of God because of corruption (1Co 15:50). The bloodline of the first man Adam cannot enter the kingdom of God, and we come through the blood of Jesus, the last Adam. Jesus blood is pure and holy and was poured out on the mercy seat for us. The life of the body of the first Adam was in the blood.

We shall have no blood in the resurrected body for the life of that body is the spirit of Christ, and we are flesh of his flesh and bone of his bone. We shall be made alive by that same Holy Spirit that raised Jesus from the dead.

1Co 15:50   Now this I say, brethren, that flesh and blood cannot inherit the kingdom of God; neither doth corruption inherit incorruption.

MYSTERY REVEALED

1Co 15:51   **Behold, I shew you a mystery; We shall not all sleep, but we shall all be changed.**

1Co 15:52 In a moment, **in the twinkling of an eye, at the last trump**: for the trumpet shall sound, and **the dead shall be raised incorruptible, and we shall be changed.**

1Co 15:53 For this corruptible must **put on incorruption**, and this mortal *must* **put on immortality.**

1Co 15:54 So when this corruptible shall have put on incorruption, and this mortal shall have put on immortality, then shall be brought to pass the saying that is written, Death is swallowed up in victory.

1Co 15:55 O death, where *is* thy sting? O grave, where *is* thy victory?

1Co 15:56 The sting of death *is* sin; and the strength of sin *is* the law.

1Co 15:57 But thanks *be* to God, which giveth us the victory through our Lord Jesus Christ.

1Co 15:58 **Therefore, my beloved brethren, be ye stedfast, unmoveable**, always abounding in the work of the Lord, forasmuch as ye know that your labour is not in vain in the Lord.

Jesus was raised victorious over death after three days and nights in Abraham's bosom, fulfilling the prophecies. Then he entered into his glory. His promise is, when he returns he will resurrect our vile bodies in the twinkling of an eye and fashion them like his own. Those who have not died will be changed in a moment also. John says that when we see him, we shall be like him for we shall see him as he is. That revelation will change us forever into his likeness, blameless and perfect.

Php 3:20 For our conversation is in heaven; from whence also we look for the Saviour, the Lord Jesus Christ:

Php 3:21 **Who shall change our vile body, that it may be fashioned like unto his glorious body,** according to the working whereby he is able even to subdue all things unto himself.

1Jn 3:2 Beloved, now are we the sons of God, and it doth not yet appear what we shall be: but we know that, **when he shall appear, we shall be like him; for we shall see him as he is.**

LIFE AFTER DEATH

Joh 11:25 Jesus said unto her, **I am the resurrection, and the life:** he that believeth in me, **though he were dead, yet shall he live:**

Joh 11:26 And whosoever liveth and believeth in me **shall never die. Believest thou this?**

Some teach that when we die, we enter into what they call soul sleep. That belief says that when we die the soul stays in the grave with the body. That contradicts the word of God. There are spirits of just men in heaven (Heb 12:23). We presently sit in heavenly places through Christ Jesus, and at death, our spirit man will leave our body and continue to live with him just as He promised. He that believes in him will never die. The spirit and soul will not wait in the grave in slumber but depart to be with Jesus in heaven. However, the body will remain in the grave until the resurrection at Christ return.

Paul said he was willing to be absent from the body and be present with the Lord. The only time we are missing from our body is at death. The body is left on earth and rest with the promise of the resurrection. At Christ Jesus return the body shall be quickened (made alive) and raised incorruptible. He will bring the spirits of those who have died back with him at his coming (1Th 4:14). He will resurrect their bodies first and then change those who are alive, and then all shall be caught up and gathered to Jesus in the clouds. It is clear from the scripture that the spirit is separated from the body at death and shall be brought back to be reunited with it. All those who dwell in Christ will experience the glory of Jesus resurrection.

2Co 5:6   Therefore *we are* always confident, knowing that, whilst we are at home in the body, we are absent from the Lord:

2Co 5:7   (For we walk by faith, not by sight:)

2Co 5:8   We are confident, *I say*, and willing rather to be absent from the body, and to be present with the Lord.

2Co 5:9   Wherefore we labour, that, whether present or absent, we may be accepted of him.

2Co 5:10   For we must all appear before the judgment seat of Christ; that every one may receive the things *done* in *his* body, according to that he hath done, whether *it be* good or bad.

Php 1:20   According to my earnest expectation and *my* hope, that in nothing I shall be ashamed, but *that* with all boldness, as always, *so* now also Christ shall be magnified in my body, whether *it be* by life, or by death.

Php 1:21   For to me to live *is* Christ, and to die *is* gain.

Php 1:22 But if I live in the flesh, this *is* the fruit of my labour: yet what I shall choose I wot not.

Php 1:23 For I am in a strait betwixt two, having a desire **to depart, and to be with Christ;** which is far better:

Php 1:24 Nevertheless to abide in the flesh *is* more needful for you.

Php 1:25 And having this confidence, I know that I shall abide and continue with you all for your furtherance and joy of faith;

1Th 5:10 Who died for us, that, **whether we wake or sleep, we should live together with him.**

Paul said he desired to depart (die) and be with Christ, but he realized that he was still needed. He said it was far better for him to depart and be with Christ. Jesus died for us that whether we are alive or dead, we shall live together with him. That means no separation from Christ at all! He will never leave us or forsake us. Hallelujah!

DEATH UNDER THE OLD COVENANT

Mat 22:31 But as touching the resurrection of the dead, have ye not read that which was spoken unto you by God, saying,

Mat 22:32 I am the God of Abraham, and the God of Isaac, and the God of Jacob? God is not the God of the dead, but of the living.

Before Christ came and made the New Covenant, no man could enter into the temple of God in heaven. This information leaves us with the question of where the Old Testament saints went after death. Where did Abraham, Isaac, and Jacob go? To God, they were still alive though they were buried a long time before Jesus was born. Jesus was speaking to the Sadducees who do not believe in the resurrection at all. In their mind, the grave was the end of a man's existence. Many today in the secular academic world and even "Christian" believe this. Jesus who is the word of God and who knows all things said there was consciousness after death; he has experienced it and he lives today.

Jesus tells the story of the rich man and Lazarus who was a beggar who asked alms at the rich man's gate every day. Lazarus died and went to paradise in Abraham's bosom in hell. The rich man died and went to the place of torment in hell. There was a gulf between the two which separated them. The rich man saw Lazarus in Abrahams bosom and asked Abraham to tell Lazarus to bring him water, even just a drop. Abraham replied that the gulf could not be crossed. They were conscious, aware of their surroundings. Those in torment shall remain there until the Great White Throne judgment where they shall be resurrected and judged according to their works written in the books.

> Luk 16:23 And **in hell he lift up his eyes, being in torments,** and seeth Abraham afar off, and Lazarus in his bosom.
>
> Luk 16:24 And he cried and said, Father Abraham, have mercy on me, and send Lazarus, that he may dip the tip of his finger in water, and cool my tongue; for I am tormented in this flame.
>
> Luk 16:25 But Abraham said, Son, **remember** that thou **in thy lifetime** receivedst thy good things, and

likewise Lazarus evil things: **but now he is comforted, and thou art tormented.**

Luk 16:26 And beside all this, between us and you there is **a great gulf fixed:** so that they which would pass from hence to you cannot; neither can they pass to us, that *would come* from thence.

When men died before Christ, they descended into paradise also called Abraham's bosom because Abraham the friend of God is our spiritual father of faith (Rom 4:16). Jesus and the thief who believed went to Paradise when they died that day. That is from where Jesus preached to the spirits in prison.

Some teach that Christ went into the judgment of fire to pay for our sins and there he was tormented by fire, Satan, and his cohorts for three days. Jesus did not teach this doctrine, and neither did the disciples. Jesus asked his Father to forgive us all, and he commended his Spirit to God, not Satan. It is finished meant that Jesus paid the debt. It is the preaching of the cross that is the power of God to save (1Co 1:8). Never do we see preached by the apostles that Christ had to suffer in hell. To teach that Christ had to endure the fires of hell is saying it was not finished on the cross. It was not enough. This teaching is in opposition to what Jesus said. Neither Satan nor his demons are in hell tormenting anyone. However, they fear the future when they will suffer the torment of the flame like the rich man. Hell was prepared for the devil and his angels, and they know it is in their future (Mat 25:41; Mat 8:29). The scripture does speak of angels held in chains in darkness. The devil could not touch Jesus in Paradise to torment him after death, and it is sure that Satan doesn't want to experience the fires of hell himself. Nonetheless, he shall be cast into the lake that burns with unquenchable fire and brimstone and tormented forever (Rev 20:10). Christ did not go into the flames of hell at death, but into Paradise. Until Jesus came, no man had ascended out of Paradise and into God's presence.

Luk 23:42 And he said unto Jesus, Lord, remember me when thou comest into thy kingdom.

Luk 23:43 And Jesus said unto him, Verily I say unto thee, To day shalt thou be **with me in paradise.**

Luk 23:46 And when Jesus had cried with a loud voice, he said, Father, **into thy hands I commend my spirit**: and having said thus, he gave up the ghost.

Joh 19:30 When Jesus therefore had received the vinegar, he said, **It is finished**: and he bowed his head, and gave up the ghost.

It is finished means to make an end, to discharge a debt. Our debt was nailed to that cross, paid in full. He defeated the devil for us on the cross at Calvary. The devil probably thought he had Jesus captive in Paradise not realizing what took place on that cross. The halls of darkness were celebrating until the gates of hell suddenly swung open, and the King of kings and the Lord of lords came through triumphing over him making a spectacle of him and his devils. Through him we also are victorious!

Col 2:13 And you, being dead in your sins and the uncircumcision of your flesh, hath he quickened together with him, **having forgiven you** all trespasses;

Col 2:14 **Blotting out the handwriting** of ordinances that was against us, which was contrary to us, and **took it out of the way, nailing it to his cross;**

Col 2:15 *And* having **spoiled principalities and powers**, he made a shew of them openly, **triumphing over them** in it.

David said in the Psalms 16 that his flesh would rest in hope because God would not leave his soul in hell, neither allow his Holy One to see corruption Peter said that this Holy One is the Lord Jesus whose body was not allowed to see corruption for he raised the third day (Act 2:27). David's soul, with the souls of all saints in paradise, was raised out of that compartment of hell by Jesus, and their flesh now rests in the hope of the resurrection.

Act 2:22   Ye men of Israel, hear these words; **Jesus of Nazareth**, a man approved of God among you by miracles and wonders and signs, which God did by him in the midst of you, as ye yourselves also know:

Act 2:23   Him, being delivered by the determinate counsel and foreknowledge of God, ye have taken, and by wicked hands have **crucified and slain:**

Act 2:24   **Whom God hath raised up, having loosed the pains of death**: because it was not possible that he should be holden of it.

Act 2:25   For David speaketh concerning him, I foresaw the Lord always before my face, for he is on my right hand, that I should not be moved:

Act 2:26   Therefore did my heart rejoice, and my tongue was glad; moreover also **my flesh shall rest in hope:**

Act 2:27   **Because thou wilt not leave my soul in hell, neither wilt thou suffer thine Holy One to see corruption.**

Act 2:28   Thou hast made known to me the ways of life; thou shalt make me full of joy with thy countenance.

Jesus first had to descend into the lower parts of the earth where the saints' abode and he preached to the spirits in prison. When he was resurrected and ascended on high, he took those who were captive in Abraham's bosom with him.

> 1Pe 3:18 For Christ also hath once suffered for sins, the just for the unjust, that he might bring us to God, being put to death in the flesh, **but quickened by the Spirit:**
>
> 1Pe 3:19 By which also he went and **preached unto the spirits in prison;**
>
> 1Pe 3:20 Which sometime were disobedient, when once the longsuffering of God waited in the days of Noah, while the ark was a preparing, wherein few, that is, eight souls were saved by water.
>
> 1Pe 4:6 **For this cause was the gospel preached also to them that are dead**, that they might be judged according to men in the flesh, but **live according to God in the spirit.**

All are judged righteously according to what they did when they lived on earth in the flesh. Those spirits in the fires of hell were wicked and were not raised. David and all who were of faith were given life in their spirit man and raised out of the lower parts of the earth after Jesus resurrection and ascension. The wicked shall remain imprisoned until the time of judgment at the Great White Throne (Rev 20:11-15).

> Eph 4:8 Wherefore he saith, **When he ascended** up on high, **he led captivity captive,** and gave gifts unto men.

Eph 4:9 (Now that **he ascended,** what is it but that **he also descended first into the lower parts of the earth?**

Eph 4:10 He that descended is the same also that **ascended** up far above all heavens, that he might fill all things.)

Rev 1:18 *I am* he that liveth, and was dead; and, behold, I am alive for evermore, Amen; and **have the keys of hell and of death.**

THE RESURRECTION

Heb 9:26 For then must he often have suffered since the foundation of the world: **but now once in the end of the world hath he appeared to put away sin** by the sacrifice of himself.

Heb 9:27 And as **it is appointed unto men once to die,** but after this the judgment:

Heb 9:28 So Christ was once offered to bear the sins of many; **and unto them that look for him shall he appear the second time without sin unto salvation.**

The first time Jesus came, it was to be a sacrifice for the salvation of the world. When Jesus returns the second time it will be for the believer's salvation: the resurrection and glorification of the saints. The Lord will deliver the body of the believer from its corruption and mortality caused by sin. Those who are looking for Christ return shall experience the redemption and glorification of our bodies which will be the finishing of our faith (Ro 8:23). Jesus is the author and the finisher of our faith. Our faith shall be finished, and we shall become established without blame in holiness. That means there will be no flaws in our character or our body whatsoever. Praise God!

> **1Th 3:12** And the Lord make you to increase and abound in love one toward another, and toward all *men*, even as we *do* toward you:
>
> **1Th 3:13** To the end he may stablish your hearts unblameable in holiness before God, even our Father, **at the coming of our Lord Jesus Christ with all his saints.**

There is comfort knowing our loved ones are alive and with Christ and will come back with him from Heaven. They will be raised from the dead first and we who are alive shall be caught up together with them in the clouds to meet our Lord. We shall always be with him.

> **1Th 4:13** But I would not have you to be ignorant, brethren, concerning them which are asleep, that ye sorrow not, even as others which have no hope.
>
> **1Th 4:14** For if we believe that Jesus died and rose again, **even so them also which sleep in Jesus will God bring with him.**
>
> **1Th 4:15** For this we say unto you by the word of the Lord, that we which are alive *and* remain unto the coming of the Lord shall not prevent them which are asleep.
>
> **1Th 4:16** For **the Lord himself shall descend from heaven** with a shout, with the voice of the archangel, and with the trump of God: and the dead in Christ shall rise first:

1Th 4:17 Then we which are alive *and* remain **shall be caught up together with them in the clouds, to meet the Lord** in the air: and so shall we ever be with the Lord.

1Th 4:18 Wherefore comfort one another with these words.

When Christ comes suddenly as a thief, it will take by surprise all those on the earth except believers in Christ. We are not appointed to obtain God's wrath, for Jesus already bore the wrath of God for those who believe in him. He shall appear the second time, not to pay for sins, but to gather from the earth all his redeemed.

1Th 5:2 For yourselves know perfectly that the day of the Lord so cometh as a thief in the night.

1Th 5:3 For when they shall say, Peace and safety; **then sudden destruction cometh upon them,** as travail upon a woman with child; and they shall not escape.

1Th 5:4 But ye, brethren, are not in darkness, that that day should overtake you as a thief.

1Th 5:5 Ye are all the children of light, and the children of the day: we are not of the night, nor of darkness.

1Th 5:6 Therefore let us not sleep, as *do* others; but let us watch and be sober.

1Th 5:7 For they that sleep sleep in the night; and they that be drunken are drunken in the night.

1Th 5:8 But let us, who are of the day, be sober, putting on the breastplate of faith and love; and for an helmet, the hope of salvation.

1Th 5:9 For God hath not appointed us to wrath, but to obtain salvation by our Lord Jesus Christ.

1Th 5:10 Who died for us, that, whether we wake or sleep, we should live together with him.

Since we know all these things beforehand let us remain steadfast and use our time wisely to grow in grace and in the knowledge of Jesus (2Pe 3:17-18). Let us hold fast the profession of our faith without wavering and exhort one another to love and do good works; for God is faithful to keep his promises (Heb 10:23-24). Our glorification will far exceed anything we could ever imagine. We shall not be disappointed.

Rom 8:18 For I reckon that the sufferings of this present time *are* not worthy *to be compared* with **the glory which shall be revealed in us**

AFTERWORD

Psa 85:6 Wilt thou not revive us again: that thy people may rejoice in thee?

(God has revived us through sending his Son Jesus Christ.)

The prayer for our revival should be prayed now by the Church, by every Christian who believes in Jesus Christ and stands in his truth.

> 2Chr 7:14 If my people, which are called by my name, shall *humble themselves, and pray, and seek my face, and turn from their wicked ways*; then will I hear from heaven, and will forgive their sin, and will heal their land.

We are not just to seek knowledge of God but a relationship with God. We are to humble ourselves, pray, and seek God's face, and turn away from all wicked ways. Many of us sought out God's word and yes, even theology which is the study of the nature of God, religious beliefs, theory and ceremonies. The book of James tells us that even the devils believe in God, yet they tremble. *When we seek his face* and build a relationship with our Lord, we will not be living a theory but a reality. Paul had a great knowledge of the law and considered himself to be a Pharisee of Pharisees, but he was ignorant of Jesus Christ (Acts 9:14; 23:6.) Knowledge will not set us free, but Jesus, the truth will. Jesus said that he is the way, the truth, and the life and he is the only path to the Heavenly Father (Joh 14:6).Learning about and seeing God's word for guidance is very important and a must, but at the same time turning away from the old ways, and being transformed by the renewing of our mind will enable us to begin our walk as a believer (Eph 5:1-21). It will help us to begin our relationship as a child of God with our Heavenly Father.

We are now ambassadors for Christ. When we have our relationship established we will then have the mind of Christ and know his will (not ours). We can then represent him which will allow the Holy Spirit to work through us. Jesus said that we shall do also the works he did and even greater (Joh 14:12). As we go out and preach the gospel, the good news of Jesus Christ everywhere, when we have relationship, the Lord will be a very present Presence! He will confirm his word through accompanying signs (signs must follow). God will revive us again and we shall rejoice in Him (Psa 85:6).

Psa 126:5 They that sow in tears shall reap in joy.

Psa 126:6 He that goeth forth and weepeth, bearing precious seed, shall doubtless come again with rejoicing, bringing his sheaves with him.

Pastor JR Beck
(Last Harvest Cowboy Church, Butler Mo.)

God has appointed you to bear fruit and that your fruit would remain that your joy would be full (Joh 15). He wills for us to grow from glory to glory. If you follow after Jesus you will succeed in all he has ordained for you to achieve, and conquer all he has appointed for you to overcome. You can make a difference by shining the light of Jesus in the darkness and revealing God's love to a world lost in sin. It is the last days, the harvest is great. Let us labor together sowing and reaping, bringing others to Christ as we vigilantly watch for our blessed Lord and Savior Jesus Christ.

Associate Pastor Lynda Sturdevant
(Last Harvest Cowboy Church, Butler Mo)

www.ingramcontent.com/pod-product-compliance
Lightning Source LLC
LaVergne TN
LVHW011933070526
838202LV00054B/4612